BY:

BEND

NANCY J. HEDIN

NO LONGER PROPERTY OF
SEATTLE PUBLIC LIBRARY

ANGLERFISH
PRESS

Anglerfish Press
PO Box 1537
Burnsville, NC 28714
www.AnglerFishPress.com
Anglerfish Press is an imprint of Riptide Publishing.
www.RiptidePublishing.com

This is a work of fiction. Names, characters, places, and incidents are either the product of the author's imagination or are used fictitiously. Any resemblance to actual persons living or dead, business establishments, events, or locales is entirely coincidental. All person(s) depicted on the cover are model(s) used for illustrative purposes only.

Bend
Copyright © 2017 by Nancy J. Hedin

Cover art: Natasha Snow, natashasnowdesigns.com
Editors: Rachel Haimowitz, May Peterson
Layout: L.C. Chase, lcchase.com/design.htm

All rights reserved. No part of this book may be reproduced or transmitted in any form or by any means, electronic or mechanical, including photocopying, recording, or by any information storage and retrieval system without the written permission of the publisher, and where permitted by law. Reviewers may quote brief passages in a review. To request permission and all other inquiries, contact Anglerfish Press at the mailing address above, at AnglerFishPress.com, or at marketing@riptidepublishing.com.

ISBN: 978-1-62649-551-7

First edition
May, 2017

Also available in ebook:
ISBN: 978-1-62649-550-0

BEND

NANCY J. HEDIN

ANGLERFISH
PRESS

For Tracy, Sophia, and Emma
And in memory of Mom, Dad, and David

TABLE OF
CONTENTS

CHAPTER ONE
THE CALL

It was early morning on a Saturday, and my momma was waking up God. Since the night before, when Momma answered a phone call, she had been beseeching God as if she had him on retainer like a lawyer or on a leash like a dangerous dog.

I stayed in my room. I would have dressed in camouflage or armor if I had any. I didn't.

"Lorraine."

Christ, I cringed every time I heard her call my name. It reminded me of everything I hated about being seventeen years old, still in high school, and living in Bend, Minnesota. Why'd I have to be called such an old-fashioned name? For that matter, why were we living like we were some hicks from the Stone Age: no cell phone, no cable TV, and no internet? I was trapped everywhere I turned.

I went to slip through the window, but before I could get completely out of the house and truthfully say I didn't hear her, Momma called me into the kitchen. She said I should explain what had possibly necessitated a call from the minister and a Saturday morning meeting about "your daughter."

"That's what he said to me, Lorraine: 'your daughter.' Who do you suppose he meant?"

"It could be Becky." I said it, but I didn't believe it for a damn minute. My twin sister, Becky, wouldn't be the subject of a serious meeting with Pastor Grind unless somebody wanted to name her a saint, and I doubted the Church of Christ went in for saints. That was more of a Catholic thing.

My momma wasn't Catholic, but she continued the inquisition anyway.

"What would people think to know I've been called in to Pastor Grind's office? Do you think it's about the scholarship? So help me God if your sister doesn't win the McGerber scholarship, I'm going to raise holy hell."

What about me winning the scholarship? That was what I wanted to say, but I didn't. I was smart enough to win a scholarship and smart enough to know I shouldn't suggest to my momma that anybody but her Becky would win it. It didn't matter that I wanted the scholarship. It didn't matter that I wanted out and needed out—out of reach of Momma; out of Bend, Minnesota; and just plain out.

I'd done what I could to earn college money. I saved every penny I made bussing tables at the diner where Momma worked. I raised chickens and rabbits and sold them. I worked with Benjamin "Twitch" Twitchell, my dad's best friend and the local vet, when Momma would allow it. I had good grades and plans to study pre-veterinary medicine in college. The librarian had helped me apply, and I had already been accepted to an animal sciences program. I hadn't told anybody. It was on a need-to-know basis, and nobody else needed to know. For that matter, the college didn't know I didn't have the money to go unless I won that scholarship, and no matter what Momma thought, I had a real shot at winning a scholarship.

Who's in trouble with Pastor Grind? I wondered. Then I wondered, *Who am I kidding?* Becky never did anything wrong. I was in trouble, sure as hell, but which sin had Pastor Grind uncovered? I went outside our farmhouse and gave myself the most complete moral frisking I could muster.

Yes, I had sold my lunch ticket for cash. Yes, I resold candy and pop from my locker between classes. And yes, boys with too many chores and sports practices and too little time and intellect to complete biology worksheets and English compositions had paid me to do their homework. Although these were sins by the book, I doubted that any of that mattered to Pastor Grind. I dug deeper—examined my heart, soul, and hormones. Holy Christ, it had to be the kiss.

I paced east to west on the open front porch and pulled at the bill of my baseball cap like the pressure against the back of my head would give me a good idea. It didn't. My dogs, Pants and Sniff, walked along beside me, their nails clicking on the floor boards. Why hadn't I kept my lust in my heart where it belonged?

The screen door slammed, Becky making her typical entrance onto the front porch. She planted herself in the porch swing with her nose in a *Good Housekeeping* magazine. She set a *Brides* magazine beside her.

"Momma's sure got her undies in a knot about something," Becky said. "What'd you do now?"

"Shut up! What do you know about it?"

"I know that it was Pastor Grind on the phone," Becky said. "I know that Pastor Grind will announce who wins the McGerber scholarship in May. And I know that the scholarship will go to the brightest, holiest student in Bend. We both know who that is, and it isn't you."

"You're right. It's probably Jolene Grind," I said, knowing that the suggestion would irritate Becky.

"She's smart, but her grades aren't as good as mine," Becky said. "That scholarship is mine. I'm going to win that scholarship and attend the Bible College in St. Paul."

"You haven't won it yet."

I tried to sound confident, but I knew that Becky stood in the way of the biggest scholarship offered in Bend, Minnesota. The McGerber scholarship, named after its benefactor, J.C. McGerber, was supposed to be awarded to the graduating senior with the highest grades, but given that McGerber was a holier-than-though-pew-polishing-member of our church, he might just choose Becky anyway. After all, Becky was a member of BOCK—Brides of Christ's Kingdom, a club for girls at our church. I had not been asked to join—not that I missed memorizing Bible verses, cooking hot dish for church socials, and knitting potholders for missionaries. What the hell did missionaries need with potholders anyway?

Becky and I had the highest grades in our class. Which of us had the fraction of a point higher, I wasn't sure. I hoped that if we were tied, the competition would be settled by a wrestling match, but the way my luck ran it would be a spirituality contest or, worse yet, a beauty contest. Becky was blonde, beautiful, and built. It was like the geometry book was divided between us. She got all the curves, and I got the angles.

I was usually quick to remind Becky that I was born first. In Biblical terms we were the Jacob and Esau of Bend. I was the hairy firstborn fixated on animals, born every bit dark as Becky was light. My brown wild curls spiraled while Becky's straight blonde tresses only curled at the ends. I expected to lose my birthright to my smoother, younger twin. Like the twins in the Old Testament story, we had competed since we were in the womb, and like the twins of the Old Testament, Momma favored the younger one.

The goal was college, but Momma didn't offer a way to pay for that goal. We were just supposed to make it there somehow. Dad wasn't any help either. He didn't believe in student loans. He wouldn't stand for them, and he wouldn't sign for them. The winner of the scholarship went to college the next fall. The loser had to stay in Bend and work at the diner where Momma worked, until she had earned enough money to go to school or just given up on college and married somebody.

If Momma knew any more details about why Pastor Grind called, she didn't tip her hand. It was like Momma tumbled the information over in her mind, polishing it like a rock. Eventually, she'd sling that stone at someone. I was prepared to duck.

Becky and I stayed busy on the front porch ignoring each other. Dad was in the barn finishing his farm chores before he left for whatever grunt construction job he'd hunted up to bring more money into our house. God, how I wished that phone had rung when only Dad had been in the house. He wouldn't have answered it. He hated the phone. He said it was a noise contraption that interrupted the thinking time of good people. Furthermore, he said it was an obsession to a whole group of people who could sure benefit from some thinking time. But Dad hadn't answered the phone. Momma had.

Then the peace was broken. Momma's voice, like a shovel scraping against concrete, carried in the humid August air and filtered out the open windows. More prayers and curses. Her habit of praying and cussing had increased since the Bend congregation had hired Pastor

Grind. Momma said she knew him from when she was a girl, and she liked his stand on sin. He was against it, and he defined it broadly. His list of for-certain sins, possible sins, and things a person shouldn't even think was longer than either the Lutherans' or the Catholics'. Momma had no time for Jesus, or as Momma called him, "the sissy god-man of the New Testament." She said Jesus was God and all, and that we should follow his word in the New Testament, but he just wasn't the man of action like the God in the Old Testament.

Momma's God wore pants, and needed to shave several times a day to keep from having a swarthy five-o'clock-shadowed face. Her God threw jagged stones at transgressors and roasted unrepentant sinners in the fires of hell. She clung to the wrathful old timer of the Old Testament who ferreted out and punished sin the way some rogue cop from the movies punished crime.

The screen door slammed, and Momma rumbled out of the house. She wore her blue dress, her church dress.

"Crap!" I mumbled.

That dress was as much of a sign as a screaming siren or a green-tinted sky before a tornado. It confirmed what I suspected—someone was in big trouble. Momma inspected Becky and me, and then she scanned the yard over the top of her glasses. Our yard attracted junk like cat hair on stretch pants. The care of the yard was the only domain I knew of that Dad had not let Momma rule. It was a rare instance, but I remembered Dad using his firm voice when he'd once said, *"Peggy, you promised that the yard was mine. I don't fight you on nothing else, but the yard is mine."*

I knew Momma wouldn't pardon Dad for the cluttered lawn he'd created. She wouldn't excuse it. She would put it in a queue for her attention another time. To that end, she removed her dog-eared, spiral-bound notebook from her purse. Her personal pencil was secured to the spiral by a piece of string. At one time, the pencil had had the golden rule printed on it, but now had been used to the point that it just read: *Do unto others.* Momma pinched the pencil between her calloused fingers, licked the lead, made a note, slapped the notebook shut, and slid it into her purse. She soldiered down the steps toward the car. "Becky, darling. Keep an eye on that roast I put in the slow cooker."

Momma didn't trust Crock-Pots.

"Lorraine, you can run to the barn and tell your dad I have a meeting at church."

Becky hoisted herself out of the porch swing and came to stand next to me, elbowed me, and we both trailed after Momma while spitting insults to each other under our breath.

"Pig."

"Cow."

"Idiot."

"Moron."

My stomach clenched like a fist. I thought about the scholarship and the kiss. My affliction compounded.

"Becky, tell your dad I'm going." Momma looked directly at me. "You might as well come along. It'll probably save me the trouble of repeating myself later. My guess, this meeting has something to do with you."

Becky giggled. I choked.

"Momma, are you sure you don't need me to drive you?" Becky called after Momma.

I rolled my eyes and discreetly flipped my middle finger at the suck-up asswipe.

"No, honey. I'll be fine," Momma called over her shoulder as she marched me to the family car.

Momma opened the driver's-side door of our ancient blue-paneled station wagon, designed for family vacations, but sturdy enough for third-world invasions. Momma wedged herself behind the steering wheel, then clawed at the seat belt and negotiated it from that dark, hidden place below her left hip. Dust, hair, and candy wrappers stuck to the sides of her hand. I kept my fingers crossed that Momma would keep hold of the seat belt and not let it speed back to its burrow between the seat and door. She needed no extra aggravation. After Momma had stretched the strap to the last inch of fabric, she forced the silver tongue into the buckle and let it settle against her stomach. *Click.*

My breakfast of Oaty Loops scrambled up my throat like it was fleeing a burning building. Only the distraction and possible danger of Momma's driving kept me from vomiting right then and there.

Backing down was impossible for Momma. Backing up wasn't her strong suit either. Momma jerked the car backward six inches or a foot, then hit the brakes. After five rounds of this, she pressed harder on the gas pedal and the car sped backward until it hit the clothesline pole.

The clothesline pole brought the car to a full stop. Momma rubbed her neck and pounded her palms on the steering wheel. The whiplash must have knocked Momma's original idea out of her head.

"Get out. Get out!" Momma yelled at me. "Just make sure I can find you when I get home." She shifted the car into drive. I didn't need a second invitation. I scampered out of the car. Momma weaved the car toward the blacktop. I stood by Becky.

"Cow."

"Horse."

"Puke."

"Shithead."

The faint smell of roast beef filtered out into the yard when Becky opened the door, entered, and returned again from checking the Crock-Pot. She turned to me. "What's that crashing sound? Oh, that's the sound of you bussing dirty plates at the diner for the rest of your life, Lorraine."

"Becky, you don't know me or what I am capable of." God, I hoped I was right, because I didn't want anyone knowing what I'd done.

CHAPTER TWO
THE KISS

In the heat of the August sunshine and impending doom of Momma and God's wrath, I allowed myself to think briefly of the kiss. I hadn't made one slip until the last week of school. I kissed her. I wanted to blame the slip up on the baseball team and fragrance-induced amnesia. The Bend Pioneers had defeated the pukes from Browerville for the conference championship. The whole school had been giddy. I'd been caught up in Pioneers fever when I'd entered the music practice room to work on my map of the Ottoman Empire with Jolene Grind.

The room usually smelled like valve oil and sweat, but that day it smelled like Jolene's Baby Magic lotion and strawberry Lip Smacker. The flowery, fruity smells went right to that part of my brain that controlled memory. I completely forgot I wasn't supposed to be queer. I wasn't supposed to secretly love Jolene, and I sure as hell forgot I wasn't supposed to kiss Jolene Grind, the daughter of Pastor Allister Grind.

But that kiss—how could anyone in their right mind find anything wrong with that kiss? When my lips touched Jolene's cheek, a cheek cool and smooth like the belly of a minnow, I shuddered and said, "Mmm."

When I opened my eyes, Jolene was staring at me like I had two heads and both of them were butt-ugly.

"What are you doing?" Jolene's eyes widened and her face flushed. "Holy Sodom and Gomorrah, Lorraine! You want to put us both on the fast train to hell too?"

I hadn't a clue what she meant by that, but I didn't say anything.

She rummaged through her quilted book bag. "Here, you hold this." Jolene handed me her *Good News for Modern Man* edition of the

Bible. Then she grabbed it back again, stuffed it in her bag, and took my hands in hers. I loved her holding my hands, but it was obvious on Jolene's face that she remembered all the things that I had forgotten. "I forgive you, Lorraine. I won't tell anybody."

Since the kiss, I had allowed myself several daydreams about how I would eventually live with Jolene Grind. Previously, I had lived off the crumbs of friendship, times when Jolene rested her head on my shoulder during long bus rides for field trips, times we cuddled close against the cold Minnesota air during late-season football games, and times when I sat by Jolene in the pew of the church where Jolene's father preached damnation for all queers like me.

Why was it that boys had to have all the girls' kisses for God to be happy? I didn't want to kiss boys. I'd enjoyed football and baseball with them in their yards and at recess when I was in elementary school. I wanted to run faster, pass farther, and tackle harder than the boys, but I never wanted to kiss boys. I'd loved girls by first grade. I didn't ask for the feelings to come, and they didn't go away. Plenty of times over the past couple of years, Pastor Grind had said that if feelings like that didn't go away, then the feeler of those feelings was going straight to hell.

Thoughts of hell burned my eyes, and tears dammed up as I looked at Jolene Grind. Even though I believed she wouldn't tell, some of me wanted to rewind, erase what happened. I was seven parts scared and eight parts embarrassed. I only half listened while Jolene spoke, searching my brain for a suitable lie for what I'd done, if anyone ever found out. Would they believe there'd been a fly on Jolene's cheek and I'd gently swatted it away with my lips?

"I'm so sorry, Jolene. I wasn't thinking. Please don't hate me."

"Lorraine, I could never hate you. But you don't know the problems your desires could make for everybody."

Jolene cried. Seeing Jolene cry made my heart break all over again, and I hated myself for what I felt and the stupid mistake I'd made. Then I shuddered for a second time. A vision of Momma flashed in my mind. She was scowling at me, wearing her blue dress hiked up along her hips, because my mistake had staked her to a big wooden cross. I hated myself. Again.

Jolene said she would pray for my soul at church. I wanted to tell Jolene that my soul could wait. I wanted to tell Jolene to pray for my body to have a place to live if Momma found out I kissed a girl. I wanted to tell Jolene if prayer helped, Momma would have prayed me into liking boys and shoehorned me into dresses and patent leather shoes ever since she had read about me loving girls in my journal. The sneak.

I prayed too, but nothing changed. That's what I wanted to scream at Jolene, but I didn't. I stayed quiet and sorry.

After the kiss, the promises of prayers, and the remorse, Jolene gathered up her stuff, touched my shoulder, and said she would see me the next day at school. Jolene never mentioned the incident to me again. The school year ended. Summer came.

Now, a new school year was about to begin and still nothing had changed. I looked around the yard and at the cloud of dust Momma had left in her wake. I knew Momma hated me for being queer. Sure, she loved me some, but Momma worried more about my salvation than my happiness.

I knew Dad knew I was homosexual, because Momma wouldn't have missed the opportunity to tell him. I wasn't certain that Dad really cared that I was queer. He probably had an animal story that evidenced the necessity of aberrant pairings for the survival of the species. To him, maybe I was just an interesting animal variation in nature. My dad had an animal story for everything. After I didn't get up for school when Momma called me and I missed the bus, Dad told me I could walk. He said that every year the wildebeests of the Serengeti migrated five hundred miles to Kenya for better grazing. He reckoned I could walk the three miles to school for the sake of my education. I told him that many of those wildebeests were killed by predators on that journey. He said he'd take full responsibility if I were eaten on the way to school.

The one time Momma had mentioned me being queer with Dad and me in the same room, Momma had sworn Dad to secrecy, but I was certain she wrote pages upon pages in her notebook, and

I suspected she even added a couple of diagrams that I was too scared to look upon.

"Once God heals Lorraine, nobody need know about her deformity," she'd said.

Hell, I figured Momma was pissed that God knew about it.

Becky knew. I took some consolation that Becky couldn't bring herself to use the words *queer* or *homosexual*. Becky wouldn't advertise it. She'd have been afraid to catch it. Besides, Becky didn't pay attention to anyone but herself and her dumb boyfriend, Kenny.

Since I'd made my kissing mistake with Jolene, Jolene knew. This brought me right back to the question of what Pastor Grind had called about. I needed to go to the barn and tell Dad that Momma had gone to the church, and then I needed to press for information from the nearest all-knowing being: Becky.

CHAPTER THREE
THE WAIT

When I returned from telling Dad that Momma had gone to the church, Becky was back on the front porch, swinging and gazing at herself in a mirror.

I just looked at Becky and wondered where she came from. "You give the roast permission to cook on its own?"

Becky didn't answer. She stared into the mirror of her compact and spackled her lips with a layer of Pepto-Bismol–colored lipstick. She licked her fingers and corralled a couple of hairs that had come loose from her French braid, which made me reach up and touch my own mop. That morning I had snared the back with a rubber band and subdued the top with a baseball cap. I pulled off my cap, the rubber band broke, and my hair sprang out from my head. "I bet you wish you had these curls."

Becky snorted. God forbid she just laugh at something I said anymore. Still, she motioned for me to sit in front of her on the floor of the porch.

I knew what that meant. She wanted to play a game we had played since we were old enough to pull hair and hold a comb. We called it "beauty school dropout." The object of the game was for Becky to make my unruly hair into some hairdo from her magazines. I didn't always like the outcome, but I always liked when Becky touched my hair.

We were shaded on the porch, but still sweating. The humidity hadn't reached the state of locker room closeness yet, but the sun had burned the dew off the grass and warmed the air to eighty degrees. Pants and Sniff plopped on the porch floor beside me when I called them. I rubbed and scratched their bellies—the pleasure loosened their joints and they flailed like they were strumming a guitar. I knew just how they felt. I was slack-jawed and nearly drooling as Becky tamed and braided my hair. That perfect moment was blown to bits when the reason for Becky's earlier primping barreled up the drive in a rusty Dodge truck. Kenny Hollister.

He was bigger than any of the boys in our class, even though he was a year younger. He wasn't bad looking if you liked boys, and Becky did. Muscled but lean, he moved like a big cat: agile and fast. He was a natural at any sport he decided to play. It was the deciding that caused a problem. Kenny joined the teams and did well at first, but then he quit—usually after a fight with another player or the coach.

Becky let out a deep sigh. "Be still, my heart."

I groaned, "Be still, my gag reflex."

Although she'd braided only half my head, she pushed me to the side, tucked her makeup case behind a pillow on the swing, and hustled to the top step of the porch as Kenny parked his truck near the house.

Becky fiddled with her already perfect hair. "Why's he got his smelly hunting dogs with him?"

Kenny loped over to Becky. She lingered on the step. Once she could reach him, she kissed him. Kenny wiped lipstick off his face but leaned in for another kiss. She burnished his face and neck with her hands, and then let her arms fall around Kenny's shoulders and kissed him again.

I had to smile. I didn't want to kiss Kenny, but I sure as hell wanted to kiss somebody like that.

In the truck cab, Kenny's dogs, Satan and Buck, barked and snarled. Pants and Sniff jumped at the truck door and barked at them. Kenny had rolled up the windows and left his dogs in the cab, their protests muted, but the truck was heating up. They fogged and smeared the windows with their breath and slobber.

"Lorraine, go get our guest some lemonade." Becky's eyes were glued to Kenny. I couldn't tell if Becky was going to kiss him again or eat him. Becky didn't take her arms away from Kenny's neck.

"Morning is more of an orange juice moment," I said.

"Fine. Get my honey some orange juice, Lorraine."

"We're out of orange juice. We just have lemonade, and I'm not going to get it. Sorry, your highness, but it's my day off." I fingered my half-baked hairdo and searched for my hat.

Becky harrumphed into the house and mumbled something. Kenny slunk a few steps closer to me and the dogs.

"You could learn a few things from your sister. Actually, you could learn a lot. She knows how to treat a man." He wiped his mouth again. Both dogs turned their bellies up to Kenny for a rub. Sniff's tongue lapped at Kenny's hands and wrists. Kenny baby-talked to the hounds, which sickened me more.

"You can't hold your licker, can you boy?" he said. "Who's a good boy?"

It infuriated me that they liked Kenny as much as they did. I credited my dogs with better judgment.

"I could get you a date with one of my cousins. Who knows, you might even enjoy yourself." He leaned over me. I smelled his Brut cologne. It barely masked the odor of his family's pig farm.

"I'd rather be autopsied alive." I shooed the dogs off the porch and stood up, facing Kenny.

"Humph. One of these days some man's going to slap your smart mouth." He ran a finger down the side of my jaw. "I just hope I'm there to see it." He winked.

I swatted his creepy hand away, but he grabbed both my arms above the elbows and squeezed. Just then Becky came out with two glasses of lemonade. Kenny released his hold on me and headed toward his truck.

"Where're you going, Kenny? I brought you some lemonade."

"Nope, can't stay. My chores are done. I'm going hunting. I'm going to run those dogs' blame feet off. I'll pick you up later."

Gravel and dust kicked up from Kenny's truck and pelted the fiberglass woodchuck diorama Dad had put in the yard the day before. Kenny sped from the yard, barely missing Twitch's Jeep coming up the drive.

Becky offered his abandoned drink to me. "God Almighty, Kenny's cute! Did you see the way his jeans fit him? I wish he didn't have to leave so soon."

"Hmm, sugar on the rim. Nice touch, sis." I took the glass from Becky. "You know Kenny, hard for him to hang around here kissing when he could be off killing something." I rubbed one of the places on my arm where Kenny's fingernails had cut into my skin. I thought of showing the marks to Becky, but it'd be pointless. Becky was unreachable when it came to seeing anything negative about Kenny. I saved myself the aggravation.

Twitch got out of his Jeep and smiled. "Hello, girls." He tipped his Twins cap at us, letting wavy brown hair brush against his forehead and cheeks for a moment before he reined it back in with his cap.

I handed him the glass of lemonade.

"Heavens, is it a margarita?"

"Nope, Becky's lemonade. What're we doing today?"

Twitch coming was the first good thing I'd seen all day. When he came for me on a Saturday it usually meant he had a job for me—drenching sheep, or pulling a calf, or neutering or spaying somebody's pet. The pay was just above pitiful, but the labor was my idea of a vocation. Momma would only let me work for him a few times a month and never if it conflicted with a possible shift at the diner. She had forbidden me from taking the full-time summer job Twitch had offered every year since I turned fourteen. No matter how many times I asked, Momma never explained why I was forbidden to work for him.

"I gotta talk with your dad, run an errand, and then I'll pick you up." He drained the lemonade and handed the glass to Becky, but looked back at me. "I like what you've done with your hair. No makeup or dresses required for this job. Come as you are. You two, hard to believe you're from the same litter." He laughed to himself and sidled off to the barn before I could kick him.

"Becky, do you really think Grind was calling about the scholarship?"

"I don't know. I wouldn't tell you if I did. It's more fun to watch you sweat." She put the drink glasses on the porch railing, stretched her neck out, and balanced her box of *Brides* magazines on the railing. "It's probably you in trouble."

She looked at me, licked her finger, and tore another blushing, blonde, boney bride from the glossy pages. "You'll never win that scholarship. There's a morality clause. Do you know what that means, Lorraine? Even if you manage to miraculously beat my GPA, which you won't, you're a queer, a homosexual. I haven't said anything about it before, but you're a freak and you'll never win!"

Becky said the words. She spit them like it was nothing, or just some shit in her mouth. She ripped out a picture of a model in a sequined wedding dress and added it to the pile on her white, satin-covered scrapbook.

Dad came around the corner of the house just in time to hear Becky's last bit of venom: "Like Momma says, the rewards of the faithful will not be squandered on the unholy. Lorraine Tyler, God will burn you in hell for being queer!"

I lowered my shoulder and plowed into Becky. I swept her off the porch onto the lawn, and rolled her down a small hill. A perfume ad pressed against my face. We broke the porch railing, two gnomes, and flattened the hollow chipmunk tableau. Air whooshed out of Becky as I landed on her at the apron of the duck pond. We swatted at each other. She screeched. I yelled from a bruised part of me that I didn't know I had.

"You take that back!" I might've drowned Becky if Dad hadn't plucked me off her.

"Calm down, Lorraine! And you, Becky, get cleaned up and I'll deal with you later!" He pointed Becky to the house. Covered in mud, Becky looked like a walking turd. I wished I had Momma's camera so I could have taken Becky's picture and submitted it to the senior yearbook committee—with the caption: *most likely to be mistaken as fertilizer.*

"March!" Dad pointed me to the barn.

I was covered in mud and duck shit. "I hate her! I'm so tired of her being perfect."

"Nobody's perfect. I've proved that to your momma over and over again." He pushed at my shoulder. "Calm yourself down. It's going to be okay."

I'd never call my dad a hugger, but that day he halfway hugged me. He pulled me into his arms and ducked down so that our eyes met. I knew his look, knew he loved me. I tried to slow my breathing and quell my tears.

He slung his arm around my shoulders again and pushed me toward the barn. "Jesus Christ! You're a mess."

"Twitch gone?"

"Yep. Sent him on his way."

Water spurted and splashed against the side of the cow trough as Dad worked the pump handle. He wet his handkerchief and wiped a clump of mud off my chin.

"Let's get rid of your mud beard first." He took another swipe at my face and rinsed the rag before he worked the mud away from my leaky eyes. "You resemble that old raccoon you brought in the house. Jesus, your momma was mad." He chuckled. "And remember how scared Becky was when the critter jumped on her lap? She don't go in for animals much." He laughed so hard he went into a coughing jag.

Dad's nostalgic inspection of my most recent battles just refueled my anger. I wanted somebody to take something from Becky for a change.

"What're you going to do to her, Dad? Will you ground her?"

"What happens to your sister isn't your concern. Your job is to worry about yourself."

"But, Dad—"

"No buts about it. You're smarter than this. That's what gets my goat."

Then he did something I loved about him, but not always when he did it to me. From his shirt pocket he took out his little notebook and scribbled *screwworm 1960* on a page and handed the note to me. Here we went again. Momma recorded sins in her notebook, and Dad wrote out homework assignments in his. I knew the drill. Research the animal at the library and figure out the lesson.

"Most maggots eat dead things." He paused, lowered his head, and squinted one eye. "The screwworm is a different animal. Learn about it and you'll know something about anger and hate." He rinsed his handkerchief again. "You know better than to fight. Get cleaned up and get to your room without ruffling Becky." He coughed hard like he did in the morning before his coffee and first filterless Camel. I worried that I might have killed him by forcing him to manage a fight that Momma would have squelched with a threat. Dad's face bloomed purple.

"There's gonna be people that got their own opinions, and you aren't strong enough to knock all of them into the mud," he said. "Although, if you tackle them like that, you probably will knock most of them down." He grinned.

He bent over with his hands on his skinny knees and let out a long breath. His eyes slid over a pile of salvaged building material. He picked up a glass block and raised it so that sunshine filtered through it and reflected a rainbow on an oily puddle of water on the ground where I toed at the gravel. He fingered a chipped spot on the corner and spit shined the smooth flat surface with the sleeve of his shirt.

I started toward the house.

"Lorraine, I love you. Your momma loves you too!"

I looked back at my dad, the person I loved most in the world. I waited. Finally, he was going to say it—that it didn't matter that I was queer. He loved me just the way I was. I wanted him to say it. I wanted somebody to say it. After God, Dad was my best shot at having somebody who still loved me if I stayed queer. I waited. Nothing. Nothing changed.

CHAPTER FOUR
THE RECKONING

C lean and dressed, but still pissed, I watched as Momma came barreling up the driveway. She flattened the pink plastic birdbath and two peony bushes before she threw the car into park. Her yelling was audible in the house as she opened the car door and swung her feet to the ground.

"Becky!"

Whatever had happened at that meeting, Momma looked to have gotten the worst of it. Her shoes were untied. A baggy roll of knee-high nylons sloshed around her grossly swollen ankles. I wondered if Momma and Pastor Grind had talked or wrestled. I wished I could have watched.

Scrubbed, dressed, and shiny again, Becky trotted out on the front porch. "What is it, Momma?"

I moved to the dining room window, where I could see and hear both Momma and poop head stink face Becky.

"Is your dad still in the barn? He's going to want to hear this." Momma huffed and puffed as she trudged to the barn. Her big hips moved under her church dress like a gunnysack of fighting cats. She had her notebook out. Momma motioned for Becky to follow her. Becky tramped behind like an obedient dog.

The urge to sneak out there and eavesdrop was strong, but I resisted. For the moment, I allowed myself the delusion that Becky might be in trouble instead of me. I did my Becky's-going-to-get-it dance, invented that moment and performed to an audience of none. After that world premiere, I came to my senses. I paced briefly and then packed. It was clear that I needed to run away. A wave of tears stormed out of my head. Who would take care of the dogs, my mice, rabbits, barn cats, and chickens? I felt like I was going to be sick. Sure, I wanted out of Bend, but only long enough to become a vet and find love. I planned to come back and live on our land my whole life. What if Bend didn't want me back if I was queer?

Tears and snot dripped on my T-shirts, sweatshirts, and jeans as I stuffed them in a bag and thought of never seeing home again. Our farm was one hundred sixty acres bisected by blacktop. Highway 12 was the equator. Like a cinched belt, it kept the north side of the farm with the big field and swamp-dimpled rolling hills of oaks, maples, and quaking aspen from sliding toward a smaller pasture, a corn field, and our share of the lake on the south side. Our house, the barn, grain bin, the pole barn, the garage that never sheltered a car, and the well house lay on the north side of the road. If I could have lifted the north side like a blanket and shaken it out, deer, raccoons, foxes, gophers, rabbits, mice, and maybe even a bobcat would have tumbled out along with the frogs, toads, garden snakes, and salamanders. I cried thinking about leaving behind those animals. I wondered how many I could stuff in my pockets.

I grabbed clothes without caring whether they were clean or dirty or even mine. My savings, which I kept wadded up in a dirty sweat sock I knew Becky wouldn't touch, added up to four hundred dollars. I put it, sock and all, in the stuff sack. I swept my arm across the dresser in one direction and pushed my deodorant, shampoo, and field guides into my bag. Next, I cleared my family pictures into the wastebasket as I thought about the woods and fields.

I left my wildlife posters on the wall on my side of the room so Becky would have to look at them until she was sure I was gone for good. I imagined Becky would replace them with posters of Bible verses or pictures of Kenny Hollister.

I thought of my dad.

Pacing, pacing. Of course Momma wanted to see Becky. Becky would now be an only child once I'd been sent off to a deprogramming camp in some wooded enclosure hidden in the lower loop of the Bible Belt. What if I cracked under the pressure and agreed to marry some pimply boy who carried his inhalers in a quilted Guatemalan shoulder bag and wore a locket with a picture of his mother?

I took a deep breath. Nothing had changed, and it didn't matter. I needed it not to matter. Dumb old Bend. Dumb old farm. I told myself that I could be a senior somewhere else and get a diploma. Maybe I didn't even need one. Dad had never graduated, and he made a living. I hoped Jolene would remember me sometimes. I wished I had time to write a poem.

As I stuffed the last of my worldly possessions into my duffel bag, Becky came into her room. I slept there too, but everyone knew it was Becky's room. Becky's face was blotchy and red and her eyes were wet and leaky like mine. She mumbled something about Jesus and stuck her tongue out at me.

"Momma and Dad are waiting for you in the kitchen. You better get out there quick." Becky had one of Dad's pocket notebook pages clutched in her hand. She tossed it in the trash.

I dragged my overpacked stuff sack along the kitchen floor behind me. Its canvas gathered dust and buffed a bit of shine into the hardwood flooring. My mouth was dry and my throat felt like I'd swallowed my set of metal jacks. I wiped my tears onto my sweatshirt sleeve, pulled off my baseball cap, and sat at the table, sneaking glances at Momma and Dad through my overgrown bangs.

"Are you coming down with a cold? Is it sinuses?" Momma squinted at me. She fished bottles of aspirin and decongestants out of her purse and held them up to me. I waved her off.

Momma eyed my stuff sack. "If that's laundry, it's two days late or five days early depending on your perspective. Either way, I'm not doing it. You can start a load yourself after our talk. There's a new box of Tide on the basement steps."

Momma gave her notebook to Dad. I coveted Momma's notebook. I was half-scared to read it, but I also believed that it had magical powers in it and that if I could write things in it, Momma would come to believe them.

After Dad took the notebook, Momma took up her other book. More precious than her notebook was her Bible. She ran her fingers over the brown pebble-grained cover. She shined the leather spine with the same mink oil I used to keep my catcher's mitt supple and waterproof.

Momma loved the Bible. She had three of them: the King James, Revised Standard, and a stand-alone version of the New Testament. She chose which one she would fondle and quote from depending on the occasion. The King James translation of the Old Testament kicked ass and trucked no excuse for bad behavior. The Revised Standard translated the Proverbs and Psalms like cool medicine for broken hearts, and the New Testament fit snuggly in her big hand so she could whack me with it when I didn't do what she told me. I was expecting a whacking.

Today, Momma petted her fetish, the Revised Standard Version, Red Letter Edition. She fanned her face with the tissue-thin pages. The God-breathed-word entered her nostrils and agitated her to blast forth, pronounce judgment. I wished that when Jesus proofread the New Testament—his words in red alongside the inconsistent stories of his disciples—Jesus would have said something loving about queers. If he had, maybe then Momma would have read it and believed it. And then, maybe her big precious book would have let her love me.

"Go ahead, Joseph," Momma said.

Dad scanned the notebook. He wiped his face with the same red bandanna he'd used to clean the mud from my face. It left a smudge of mud and duck shit across his forehead. He stared at Momma, but she didn't look at him. Momma licked her thumb and rubbed at a spot on the table.

"For Christ's sake, Peggy, do we have to make a big deal about this?"

"Language, Joseph. Go ahead, dear, it's all in the notebook there." She folded her hands over the gold-embossed print of her Bible.

Dad stood and read mechanically from the notebook. "First of all, I need to say that I don't want you teasing Becky. Your sister and the Hollister boy like each other. In the course of their prayer time together—" He frowned, sighed, and gave Momma a pleading look. Momma's eyes were closed as she gently nodded to the cadence of him dutifully reading the script she had prepared. She stopped rocking whenever Dad stumbled on the words or stopped like he couldn't read another line.

Hollister boy? Prayer time? My head was full of bees. Shit! What about the kiss? What about Jolene?

"They've been doing it in the back of Kenny's truck! If Becky gets herself a baby, she'll forfeit that scholarship." Dad dropped back into his chair.

As the last words gushed from Dad's mouth, he slid the notebook across the table where it bumped against Momma's Bible. That wasn't what was written in the notebook because Momma opened her eyes, blushed, and glared at Dad.

The big F word, *fornication*. That was what the meeting had been about. Fornication. That was what Pastor Grind would have called it. Somebody knew or suspected that Becky and Kenny were already having sex, and they wanted our parents to know. If Becky got pregnant, she couldn't win the scholarship.

Momma swooped up her notebook and clutched it to her breast. She looked at Dad for a split second and then she sighted me in. "What your dad means is that we want you children to graduate high school and not get into anything before you're ready. Being a momma just out of high school is no picnic." Momma knew this from experience.

Momma jotted in her notebook. "Remember once you marry them and have their babies, you're stuck with them until death." She jotted a note in her notebook. "You kids can love anybody you want."

That pronouncement got my attention, but Momma immediately shut the door on any notion I had that it was okay that I loved girls. She looked straight at me.

"There're lots of nice boys in this town."

I looked at Dad. He glanced at me. I forbid my eyes to cry anymore. Did Dad feel like Momma? Did he view marriage as a death sentence too? Did he want me to notice the nice boys? I thought of the glass block, chipped, not perfect. He didn't say anything. He just turned away and let Momma go on. The yard was his. We kids belonged to Momma.

Momma shook her finger at me and tilted her head down. "With loving comes hard work and sacrifice. I had dreams too. I wanted to be a nurse." She rocked in her chair a couple of beats, lost in her thoughts. "We want you two girls to get your education before you take on all the burdens of this world and watch your dreams dissolve like mist."

Marriage and parenting was Momma's cross to bear, and by God she made sure the rest of us got a few slivers from that big wooden burden. Dad squirmed in his chair with slumped shoulders. My heart receded somewhere deeper in my chest, less exposed to the elements. The hate I felt for Momma had already gnawed a big hole in me, and I didn't care. How was it that Momma had the right to deal out burdens and sacrifices for all of us? What did Dad really think? Was he satisfied with his sacrifices?

For the second time that day I felt kind of tender toward Becky. Becky could be a shit, but no one wants to be told there's something wrong about them loving somebody.

After I was paroled from the table, I lugged my pack back into the bedroom. It wasn't yet noon, but Becky was already in bed on the top bunk facing the wall, her red gingham-checked bedsheet snugged up to her neck. All I could see was Becky's hair wrapped tightly around pink sponge rollers. I suspected that Becky was faking sleep. My hand hovered in the air near Becky's shoulder, but I didn't risk touching her. I rested my hand on the frame of the bed.

"You need me to get you anything, Becky?"

"I don't need anything from you, you freak!"

"Glad to know you're feeling more like yourself."

Before I left the room, I fished the notebook page from the trash. Dad must have given it to her. It read, *Gestation periods of rabbits, humans, and elephants.* I crumpled it up again and replaced it in the trash.

I grabbed my work boots and gloves from the mudroom and went outside to wait for Twitch. I saw him talking with Dad in the barn. As I stretched in the sunshine, I gave the farm a pretend hug. It was good to know I could always take refuge with Dad and Twitch. I had escaped Momma's and God's wrath another day, but part of me knew it was only a matter of time before Momma took aim and fired again.

CHAPTER FIVE
THE VOCATION

My dad and Twitch had been friends since they were just boys, and the way I heard it, they were virtually inseparable until Dad married Momma. Since then, they had remained good friends and rarely a day went by without Twitch stopping at our house, or Dad meeting Twitch someplace. That day the two men stood by the barn, yelled, gestured with their hands, and nearly looked at each other. Their odd deportment made me run to hear what they were saying.

"All I'm saying, you dumbass, is there's more than one way to skin a cat." Twitch spit chewing tobacco on the ground by Dad's boot.

"That's a fine expression for a veterinarian. Lorraine's not working full-time for you or taking your money. I'm her father. I will take care of my children. If I wouldn't let them take a government loan, why would I have either of them owing you?" Dad threw down his cigarette and rubbed it out with the toe of his boot.

Twitch waved at me and pointed his finger at Dad. "You are the goddamned stubbornest son of a bitch I've ever known."

I guess Dad noticed me then.

"Jesus Christ, watch your language in front of my daughter."

Twitch rolled his eyes and headed toward his Jeep. He looked in my direction. "Are you working with me?"

I nodded, but at the same time listed toward my dad. "What was that all about?"

"Tell me what you know about sheep," he said.

"Well, sheep are ruminants with four digestive chambers. They need both pasture and hay. Ewes come into heat on average every sixteen days and there is a thirty-hour window for getting bred.

Gestation's about twenty-one weeks. Dogs and coyotes are their worst enemies. Farmers raise them for meat and wool."

"That's my girl. What kind of problems do sheep have?"

"Besides going astray?"

Dad frowned.

I listed the parasites and diseases I knew and even offered to get more specific about the treatment of worms.

He shook his head. "You're a show-off! Go ahead and help Twitch. See if you can learn something from that old fool."

I got in Twitch's Jeep and asked what work he had for me.

"Well, I got a prize-winning ram in the back of my Jeep. What does that tell you?"

"It tells me you have some strange habits. You need to get out more. Most people collect stamps or coins or baseball cards."

"Anybody ever tell you you're a smart-ass?" Twitch spit some chewing tobacco out his Jeep window and wiped his chin.

"I've been called many names and smart-ass is one of the better ones. As for having a prize-winning ram in your Jeep, I'm guessing some farmer's ewes are in heat and they want you to breed them with this ram's special sauce." I flexed my brain for Twitch's benefit. "People raise sheep for milk, wool, or meat. Different breeds are known for their production and quality of product. The system of breeding is determined by the farmer's goals for his flock. There's pure-breeding, inbreeding, outbreeding, crossbreeding . . ."

"I'm impressed. Keep this up and you could actually become a veterinarian. Or a sheep." Twitch poked me in the ribs. "Actually, you're going to get some practice with crossbreeding sheep. That's why I was over this morning. I talked Holcum into pasturing his sheep and goats at your place starting next month. I got your stubborn father to agree to it finally. You can meet some of your new tenants today."

"Dad tell you all hell broke loose today?" When I was with Twitch my language matched his.

"Define *hell*."

"Well, it seems that Miss Becky Tyler's been seen fornicating with pigheaded Kenny Hollister. Pastor Grind told Momma, and there was a big family conference."

"Who told Grind?"

"I don't know. Never even thought about it." It was a good question. Who had seen Becky and Kenny? Who had told Pastor Grind?

"Well, being seventeen, in love, and having my pastor and my folks commenting on my business sounds like hell to me."

I loved Twitch for lots of reasons, but could have loved him for that statement alone. I waited until I couldn't wait anymore and asked Twitch about his fight with Dad.

"It looked like you and Dad were wrangling before we left."

"Every month I ask the old mule to let you work with me full-time or let me help you pay for vet school. Goddamn it, I have a few dollars." He looked over at me. "Does my cussing corrupt you?"

"Shit, no."

"Jesus Christ, that's a load off my mind."

"Why won't he let me work with you? He knows I want to be a vet more than anything."

Twitch didn't answer right away, which tipped me off that like most adults, he was thinking of a lie or at the very least a selective way of telling the truth.

"He's proud. He doesn't want to be beholden to me for anything," he said. "He's your dad, and he doesn't want anybody else horning in on that."

"Well, I don't know why me doing what I want is any threat to Dad. You're not too bad an influence."

Twitch pulled his Jeep into Holcum's sheep farm and parked by the barn. Ten black-faced, black-legged Suffolk sheep looked up from their pens.

"Take your gloves and notebook and check 'em for what ails them, write it down. I'll be back in a half hour or so to hear your report. Then we'll introduce them to Mr. Studley Do Right and get this party started." Twitch checked his teeth in the side mirror, hitched up his jeans, and headed to the farmhouse. Mrs. Holcum answered the door, and Twitch went inside.

It'd been most of an hour before Twitch returned to the barn. I had checked those ten sheep stem to stern, wrestled that ram down a makeshift ramp out of the Jeep, and introduced him to his ewes in waiting. That horny ram had mounted nearly every ewe by the time Twitch returned and had his gloves on.

"You started? Shit! Did the ram mount any of the ewes yet?"

"Are you kidding me? That horndog mounted just about everyone and some he mounted twice. Why? Isn't that what we were here to do?"

"Well, yes and no." Twitch took off his hat and wiped his forehead on his sleeve. He seemed to have worked up a sweat even though it was that ram and I who'd done most of the work. "There was at least one ewe Holcum wanted off-limits. He has another ram for her. It's okay. I'll talk to him later. He's not home right now, just his wife."

"Why aren't you married?" I packed up the equipment and led that Casanova ram back to the Jeep.

"Me or him?" Twitch nodded at the ram.

"You."

Twitch's eyes bugged open. "Wow, where'd that come from?"

"So, what's your answer? Why isn't there a Mrs. Twitch?"

"Are you proposing to me?"

I shoved his shoulder. "Come on, you can tell me the truth."

"I know I can. I want to tell you the truth. The truth is important."

"Well?"

"The truth is the best ones are taken or too smart to take up with the likes of me." He opened the door on my side of the Jeep. "Besides, I got everything I want without having to marry anybody."

"You and Dad are a lot alike, and he found somebody to love him, though I wouldn't recommend his taste in women. I'm not so certain why he's as crazy in love with someone as ornery as Momma."

"Goddamn, they were made for each other. Didn't he tell you how they met?"

"Yeah, yeah. They met at the diner. Blah, blah, blah. It lacks romance in my mind."

"Well, that's fine. It just had to be romantic in their minds, and goddamn if it wasn't. I was there. Ask him about it. He gets so gooey telling it. Your momma turned quite a few heads when she came to Bend." Twitch pulled on the brim of my baseball cap. "How about you? You found some boy that makes you all gooey?"

"Nope." I got back in the Jeep.

"We've got one more stop." After he'd filled the Jeep with dust from fifteen minutes of bad roads he called "short cuts," Twitch signaled a turn off the blacktop and snaked up the driveway to Kenny Hollister's place. It was a farm about the size of our farm, but with fewer trees and more outbuildings. Two single-level pig barns flanked a beat-up trailer. The main house was a story and a half. It needed paint just like the garage and outbuildings that dotted the yard. The shit-and-dust-covered machinery was sheltered under a large carport to the west of the main house.

Twitch frowned and wagged his head. "Kenny called me all excited because he won a sow in a fight with some kid. Now the sow had her litter and they don't look right."

Twitch parked his Jeep by the main house and went up to the door. Mrs. Hollister opened the door before Twitch knocked. I followed him. I had hoped to get a glimpse at Mr. Hollister. I'd heard that not only were the Hollister folks old, but Mr. Hollister was kinda demented. I'd never seen an honest to God demented person. I peeked around Twitch and beyond Mrs. Hollister, but I couldn't see the old man. Mrs. Hollister told Twitch that Kenny was hunting, and pointed him to the barn where the sick pig was.

There, in a small pen, a sow was lying on her side. She wasn't moving. Perhaps she was spent from delivering, but that didn't explain how weak and tired the baby pigs appeared. They were clean, rosy pink with a dot of iodine on a two-inch plug at their navels. One or two seemed normal, but the rest of the eight piglets dragged their hindquarters.

"What's wrong with them?"

"Probably brucellosis," Twitch said. "It's caused by a bacterium. That sow was probably infected, and the kid didn't mind losing it to Kenny. Kenny shouldn't have added the pig to his herd."

"What's the recommended treatment?" I asked.

"There is no treatment now. All you can do is put them out of their misery."

"It looks like those two piglets are okay."

"Nope, if one's got it, they've all got it, or are getting it. That's just the way nature works sometimes." Twitch glanced at me. "You okay?"

I lied and said I was, but I couldn't wrap my head around one sick baby making the whole litter worthless. It was one thing to raise animals with the eventual outcome of being slaughtered, but this horrible illness just seemed wrong.

Twitch left the pigs in the pen and told Mrs. Hollister to have Kenny call him first thing when he got home and to keep those pigs separate from the others.

"He going to have to kill 'em?" she asked.

"Yeah, I'm afraid so," Twitch said.

"Well," she arched her eyebrows and smirked. "He's good at that."

CHAPTER SIX
BIRTH CONTROL

After Momma and Dad had learned that Becky and Kenny had been having sex, they'd herded Becky and me into family activities. It was a long fall of school and homework followed by Monopoly, Risk, Sorry, pinochle, hearts, and canasta. During Momma's idea of a scavenger hunt, I located a missing set of car keys, seven stray socks, and the source of the sour smell that was coming from the southwest corner of the basement: cheese.

For those months, Momma didn't yell about the junk that filled the yard: cars, the aluminum, the copper pipe, the fish house, the broken bicycles, and eight lawn mowers that together didn't have enough working parts to get the lawn mowed regularly. For that time, our family pretended that beating each other at board games was an effective form of birth control.

Momma and Dad never forbade Becky from seeing Kenny. Becky saw him every day at school, but if they wanted to go someplace after school hours, Momma made me go with them. I lost sight of who was being punished, and most times I also lost sight of Becky and Kenny.

They traipsed off into the woods when it wasn't too cold or raining. Sometimes, they made me leave the truck so they could make out there. Usually I was glad for the brush off. It gave me time to dream, read, memorize animal facts, or sketch animals from my field guide.

Occasionally, they went to the library, telling the boldfaced lie that they were going to study. Instead, they hid and made out in the stacks. A girl I'd never seen before nearly tripped over them as they smooched and talked baby talk by the arts and crafts section. The girl was beautiful, but I didn't know if I'd ever see her again, because the library was not Becky and Kenny's favorite haunt.

Kenny had quit football or was kicked off the team, depending on who I asked. The story I heard more than once was that Kenny had blindsided one of the scrawny sophomore boys and broke the boy's collarbone in two places. Either way, the end result was that Kenny had Friday nights free.

One Friday night when Kenny came to pick up Becky, Momma pushed me out the door with them and yelled, "Lorraine will be your chaperone, kids. Be home by 10 p.m."

Becky and Kenny both glared at me.

"Don't look at me. I don't want to go with you." I had planned to take the fan bus to watch our football team humiliate or be humiliated by Upsala, but Momma had said I needed to stick with Becky and Kenny.

It was raining like a tantrum from God. I clung to the passenger door. Becky straddled the gearshift and made kissy noises at Kenny and prodded him about where he was taking her like he was possibly taking her to Fiji. Kenny pulled the truck onto the service road by the football field. Since the team was playing an away game that night, the place was deserted. Becky and Kenny had barely put the truck in park before they were all over each other.

Their pawing and panting made me glad to take my chances with the thunderstorm. I grabbed Kenny's flashlight off the dashboard and took a veterinary science book I'd borrowed from Twitch and my mammal field guide.

"Honk the horn when you're ready to leave." I left the truck and slammed the door for effect.

The roof over the bleachers was useless because the rain was coming down sideways. I passed around the front of the bleachers to the concessions building and the broadcast booth, a thin two-story building that looked like a giant box of saltine crackers covered in aqua galvanized steel. It was padlocked, but the screws on the hasp were stripped. Without much effort, I slipped into the shelter, pocketed the padlock, and pulled the door closed behind me.

My eyes adjusted to the darkness and the tunnel of light the flashlight gave me. I heard mice scatter. The floor was speckled with their scat. Mice, the universal kibble. Nearly every other animal was a predator to them, even some insects. At the same time, mice were baby factories; they had twelve to twenty-four litters a year with an average of twelve babies in each litter. I thought about Becky. Maybe Becky wanted to be a baby factory too. What about going to college? Becky had wanted to go to Bible College and study Greek and Hebrew, which made no sense to me, but more sense than staying in Bend and having babies.

A wooden ladder led to the loft where the radio announcers would broadcast the Bend Pioneers games to a meager masochistic listening audience. I climbed the ladder and made my way to the sports desk. A hook and eye kept the hinged shutter closed. I popped the hook and glimpsed at the weather. The rain had let up, and the clouds had parted. The scant fall daylight streamed in, but wasn't enough to read by. I hooked the shutter closed again and shined the flashlight on my book.

I was reading about treating abscesses in goats when I heard Becky and Kenny laugh as they stumbled into the concession area below. *Crap!* I turned off the flashlight and pressed myself against the far wall of the loft above them. I hoped I was enough in the shadows that they wouldn't discover me. From the way they were absorbed with each other, they probably wouldn't have noticed a marching band. If love was blind, then lust was downright deaf and blind. They had no notion that anyone else got in there ahead of them. Where the hell did they think I was in this storm? Maybe that was the thing about lust: you didn't care about any other person.

There was no way I wanted to be a captive audience for Becky and Kenny's making out, but how the hell was I supposed to get out of there without them noticing me? Of course worrying about them seeing me had been my error in thinking. There was only one door. Instead of announcing myself and going back to Kenny's truck, I had panicked and hid. I clutched my books and tried not to stare, but it was like a car accident. My eyes were drawn to the wreckage, and I could see and hear everything.

Kenny spread a blanket from his truck onto the floor of the concession stand and positioned his camping lantern close by. Becky stood with Kenny in the yellow-orange glow of the lantern.

"You smell so good." Kenny buried his face into Becky's hair.

"Stop it now. Maybe we should've just stayed at my house and studied tonight. Kenny, I can't take that English test for you."

"Who cares if I fail that dumb test?" Kenny's hands patted her back like he was measuring her bones for slope and angle.

"I care. You've to graduate high school before you can join me at college. Besides, you're going to care because it'll pull down your average, and that means no spring baseball." Becky pushed Kenny away weakly.

"What say I practice getting round those bases right now?" Kenny clasped his hands behind Becky's back and pulled her to him in a bear hug, until their faces were so close they had to close their eyes to kiss or be cross-eyed. "You are so beautiful, Becky." He loosened his hold on her and swept some stray hairs away from her face, barely touching her skin. "I promise to always protect you and be a man for you. That's more important to me than graduating or sports or anything I can think of in this world."

Becky looked into Kenny's eyes and put her fingers flat against her mouth. "This is what love's supposed to feel like, isn't it?"

Kenny dug condoms out of his front pocket. He told Becky how he doubted his dad needed them anymore. Kenny held the foil-wrapped envelope between his teeth as he enacted a brief striptease for Becky. He popped the pearl snaps from his Western shirt. His hairless chest shone white in the lantern's light. He kicked off his cowboy boots, and dropped his faded jeans. His white briefs and tube socks nearly glowed. Kenny fumbled with Becky's clothes and dropped them to the floor.

Goddamn it. She was wearing my lavender tank top. I gasped, covered my mouth, and nearly gave up my position when I saw that Becky's bra and panties were fire-house red, in contrast to the regulation white briefs Momma bought for us from J.C. Penney.

Becky was beautiful. Her breasts were bigger than Kenny's hands, and her hips spun out from the small oval of her waist. Her legs looked long, muscled at the thigh and calf. I wanted new underwear.

Kenny and Becky kissed and caressed each other and lowered themselves to the blanket without even stopping kissing. It wasn't long before they were both panting. I covered my eyes with my hands, but peeked between my fingers. I'd never actually seen sex between people before.

Sex education in Bend, Minnesota, was a grainy filmstrip in fifth grade showing a cartoon girl combing her hair in front of her mirror waiting for her period to come and make her a woman. I remembered how the diagram of the female reproduction system had looked like a deer skull with droopy antlers. Don't even get me started on what happened when the junior high home economics teacher, who had an awful case of rosacea on a good day, had nearly self-combusted the morning she'd showed us a big plastic sculpture of the male parts. I didn't want anybody to approach me with anything that looked like that. Becky didn't seem to have the same reservations.

Kenny rolled to his side and unwrapped a condom. Becky waved him off like he didn't need one. He gasped something about pulling out, and he entered her and started pumping away. When he started to shove off of her, she clung to him tighter and looked into his flushed, feverish face.

"It's okay," Becky said. "God told me. It's really okay, Kenny, I want you."

Kenny puffed and grunted and clawed and sobbed and came. Becky was like a live trap, and he seemed caught. Spent, Kenny collapsed on Becky's breast as Becky rocked him.

Shit. Breeding farm animals was interesting, but it was nothing close to this. I wished I could have given them their privacy. I had no right to be part of their love.

Afterward, Becky and Kenny dressed silently, turned away from each other. Kenny gathered up the blanket and lantern, and they left the concession stand.

CHAPTER SEVEN
THE ANNUNCIATION

The pill would have outperformed Momma and Dad's lecturing, planned activities, and my impotent chaperoning. Around Christmas, Becky and Kenny told Momma and Dad that Becky was two months pregnant. The two lovebirds sat at the kitchen table. Momma poured some coffee for herself and Dad. She got some milk and peanut butter cookies for Becky and Kenny.

"Go pet a beaver or something," Becky said to me. I hovered at the periphery.

After hearing that she was about to be a grandmother, I had expected Momma to blow a gasket and maybe invoke some sort of plague on Becky for getting pregnant. I waited. She didn't. Momma congratulated them and asked all the usual questions like it was just another ordinary thing in her day. When was Becky due? July. How was she feeling? A bit queasy, but pretty good.

After Kenny left there were some martyred sighs, but Momma didn't rant or lecture or do anything interesting other than jot a few notes in her notebook. Maybe Momma still smarted from her parents' reaction to her pregnancy just out of high school. Still, I expected Momma to give as good as she'd gotten. Wasn't that the conflict that kept us from visiting Momma's one remaining parent along with the four-hour drive? Wasn't excommunication a family tradition when a child disappointed a parent? I felt like I was always close to being exiled to the desert, forgotten the way Momma had forgotten her momma.

"Well, we're going to have a little one around here again," Dad said. "You know, I always planned to have a dozen—any more kids than that and I didn't think we had enough experience. Then you girls were born and your momma and I thought, why mess with perfection? The other ten couldn't be nearly as interesting."

Momma waved at me to join them at the table, then she told Becky and me stories about our time in her womb.

"It was like you were both writing on the walls."

I pictured Becky's measured script massaging a note inside Momma's body. I figured I'd probably carved my thoughts, scraped at Momma from the inside the way I grated at her outside of the womb.

"I worried you wouldn't be strong enough for the trouble of the world, Becky. And Lorraine, I worried you'd make the trouble."

Becky's pregnancy required planning. Dad made a crib for the baby, and Momma made Becky and Kenny get married, not that it took much arm-twisting for Becky. Like Momma, Becky liked the pageantry. Pastor Grind urged Becky to make that pageantry occur as quickly as possible or he would not officiate. Becky promised Momma and Dad she'd finish high school if they signed for her to get married before our eighteenth birthday in June. They agreed and approved a January wedding.

All those magazines Becky had read probably gave her romantic ideas about dresses from a bridal store in St. Paul, but Pastor Grind's time schedule forced Becky to settle for a trip to the St. Wendell shopping mall. I would have preferred hanging out at the pet store, the video arcade, or even J.C. Penney rather than the dress shop, but Momma threatened to release my pet mice and roast my chickens and rabbits if I didn't pick out a dress to wear to the wedding. Dress shopping with Becky was bad enough, but even worse because she invited her closest girlfriends to meet her there. They were my classmates, but they were Becky's friends. Where two or more of Becky's friends were gathered, you had a coven.

Through the remaining days of school before the wedding, Becky was literally a blushing bride and had showed no shame about her pregnancy. She wore tented blouses and elastic waist skirts. When she spoke to me at all it was to ask if her breasts looked bigger, which they didn't. I suggested her head and ass had swelled appreciably, but during that time period even I couldn't flap Becky. The moment for which Becky was born had finally arrived. She was about to be a bride and mother. Becky had two-timed Jesus.

CHAPTER EIGHT
THE MIRACLE

The worst part of Becky being pregnant and preparing to marry Kenny Hollister was that it took all of Momma and Dad's attention. The best part of Becky being pregnant and preparing to marry Kenny Hollister was that it took all of Momma and Dad's attention. I was under their radar. I worked with Twitch whenever I wanted. I read veterinary science and sketched whenever I wanted. Then in January, a week before Becky's wedding, it happened. I found out I wasn't the only queer in the world, and not the only queer in Bend, Minnesota.

Of all places, it happened at the most sacred ground in my hometown—second only to the woods on our farm—the library. I was there to research a stack of notebook assignments from Dad and I'd picked up our family's requests for reading that week. Momma wanted a book on the lives of the Saints, Dad wanted that book about the guy who lived alone in Alaska, Becky wanted a book on the benefits of eating the placenta, and I wanted something on raising chickens with big breasts for big profits.

I saw her again. Backlit by dusty fluorescent bulbs and stacks of musty volumes of Reader's Digest Select Editions. The newcomer pretty girl sparred with the librarian, Gerry, like gunslingers in a Western movie. I nearly sprained my ears eavesdropping.

"I have two college courses I must complete by correspondence. I was a bad girl at college," she told Gerry. "I'll need some reference materials—some that the library probably has and some other things that'll have to be borrowed from a bigger library system, and I'll need time on the library's computer."

Gerry, keeper of the books and all things Dewey Decimal, pushed her glasses back up her nose, tapped her felt-tip pen against her lip, and gave the librarian's version of the Miranda rights.

"You must have a library card to use the computer or reference department or order materials. You must have a valid picture ID to get a library card. You may only use the computer in the reference department for one hour per day if there are persons waiting to use the computer in the reference department. You may not use the computer or reference department for any illegal or immoral activities or you will forfeit all future use of the computer, reference department, and your library card."

The woman gave Gerry a puzzled look. "No immoral activities when you're giving me a whole hour in there?"

I liked that girl's spunk. I especially liked seeing that spunk wrapped up in that body.

Gerry gasped and nearly sucked her pen into her throat.

The girl smiled. "I can live with those rules, but I wish you could be more flexible on the time limit. Do you ever make exceptions?" She tilted her head to read Gerry's name tag. "Gerry?"

Obviously, she did not know nor had she heard about Gerry. I hoped I would be the one who enlightened her about the strange and curious ways of Geraldine Narrows, the Bend librarian.

I planned to point at Geraldine Narrows and note her all-season matching organic cotton skirt, vest, and suit coat, her buttoned-to-the-neck blouses noosed by complementary silk ties with petite flower or rodent patterns. She always wore hose and a sturdy tie shoe in varying shades of concrete. Geraldine had never married, and to my knowledge had never dated, lusted, or felt particularly warm about anything other than books and the machination of the Bend library. Geraldine lived in her house on our road, sandwiched between our farm and Kenny Hollister's family farm.

I trusted Gerry. She was reliable as cotton. I liked her rational approach to problem solving, her access to information, and that Gerry often helped with a school project or practical advice when Momma's mood necessitated safe distance. Hell, even Becky liked Gerry because Gerry held the newest women's magazines aside for Becky to see first. Becky helped Geraldine by sewing some of her clothes and by cooking a hot dish for Gerry every so often, because Becky said Gerry only cooked from boxes.

Most recently, Gerry had helped me review college programs in animal science. From my frequent dealings with Geraldine, I knew her to be a kind, knowledgeable, and helpful person once she got to know you, but she also liked protocol. Nothing about Geraldine suggested that she made exceptions. That was what I would tell the prettier-than-horses young woman if I ever got the nerve to talk to her.

Gerry licked her fingers, retrieved a red form, and placed it on the counter without breaking eye contact. "Yes. It's short for Geraldine, and no, I do not make exceptions. I do not have that sort of authority, but if you would like me to present your concern to the library board, you can submit a library board concern form to me. It must include your library card number."

"I guess I'm going to need a library card." The girl took a driver's license from her back pocket and placed it in front of Gerry. "How long does it take to get a library card?"

Gerry took her pen and let it tumble between the fingers of her right hand, gambler-style.

"The processing of library card requests varies depending on the volume of requests and the general work load for library staff. I will take a copy of your ID while you complete a library card request form and submit your completed paperwork to the library card issuance officer."

Still twirling the pen and looking into the girl's eyes, Gerry retrieved a goldenrod-colored form from below the desk and placed it before her. At the moment the form hit the counter, Gerry flipped her pen in the air, caught it, and presented it to the girl. The girl presented her ID to Gerry.

The duel was suspended. Gerry peered at the ID, varying its distance from her nearsighted orbs like she was playing the slide trombone. "Is this your current address?"

"God, no. Not unless we're in a suburb of St. Paul, which we clearly are not. My parents moved here a couple years ago, only God knows why. My father believes he has a direct line to God. I came here at their extortion. I haven't yet had an opportunity to change the address because I hope that my stay is only temporary. But I'll change it rather than having to take some sort of test to show I can drive a tractor or avoid stray cattle and hogs, which seem to find their way onto the roads and move faster than the motorists here," she said in one breath.

She took Gerry's hands and turned them over so that the ID fell flat onto the counter. Still holding Gerry's hands, she said, "Gerry, look at this picture."

Gerry nodded her head, never looking away from the girl's face.

"It is me. The license is reasonably accurate except for the address, and I'm much more charming in person than that picture could ever suggest." She leaned in, pulled Gerry closer. Gerry was slack-jawed. "Couldn't you see your way clear to pass my paperwork along to the library card issuance officer?"

Her lips were pouty. God how I hoped I'd have something that girl needed or wanted. Gerry couldn't lift her shield of rules anymore. Gerry photocopied the ID and slid a fresh library card across the counter a few minutes later.

"Congratulations, Ms. Charity Krans." She gave a slight salute.

Charity thanked Gerry and told her she'd be back at six thirty that evening.

She walked over to the reference area and stood on the opposite side of the glass window from me. She tapped on the glass, smiled, winked, and left the library. I was so befuddled that I dropped the *S* volume of the World Book Encyclopedia on my foot. I saved my remaining twenty-two minutes of time on the library computer in the reference department and planned to return that evening and make it an offering to Charity.

Gerry shuffled through the papers Charity had completed, while I hovered. Finally, Gerry looked up at me.

"She's new, huh?"

"Yes," Gerry said. "She never actually lived here with her folks before. She stayed in St. Paul. College, I suppose. That's Grind's oldest daughter. They don't talk about her much. She changed her name."

"Holy shit! Oops, sorry I swore."

"Holy shit indeed. Hard to believe she's related to that minister, isn't it? No offense. You go to that church, don't you?" Gerry took her papers over to the typewriter.

"You think she got married?"

"No. I heard she just changed her name," Gerry said. "Even her first name. She used to be Jeannine or something like that. That family has a thing for J names—probably would have named a son Jesus."

Gerry let me use the library phone to call home for a ride. I wanted to get home to take a bath, wash my hair, and find the right clothes for seeing Charity again. I hoped Dad would drive me to the library again later. At the same time, I was resolved to walk to the library if Dad wouldn't take me.

There was no good reason to expect that another person like me existed in my own town and that she could be beautiful and also need the library. My heart raced and my mind tried to keep up. Something told me that Charity Krans hadn't noticed the nice boys in town either. Maybe it was like elephants. Elephants tapped the ground and communicated to other elephants miles away. Maybe all this time the yearnings of my heart had reverberated—tapped the ground. Maybe Charity had heard me and come in my direction. I kept my ear to the ground.

Charity was already at work by the time I reached the library. I watched her as she thumbed through reference books, made notes, and rat-a-tatted on the computer keyboard. This wasn't the entrance I had pictured. I had planned to be there first, seated in the reference section. I imagined that Charity would have stood close to me and asked whether the other seat in the reference section was taken. I had planned to look up at Charity with my brown cow eyes and high cheekbones—the only thing my momma gave me worth mentioning. I'd intended to drink Charity in. I'd planned to tell Charity that I had saved most of my time on the computer so that I could give it to her because I'd heard she needed to get her college course work done.

In my mental romance Charity smiled at me, asked my name, and discovered that at least somebody in this one-horse town knew she had important things to do. I imagined Charity seated in a chair next to me.

Lust oozed from my heart, lust for someone who was like me, lust for someone who would like me, lust for knowing what it would be like to like somebody like me who liked me back. I had lust in my heart and impatience in my soul. I was impatient thinking of how all the dumb boys clumsily flirted with girls, went places with them, held their hands, and kissed them.

Lust and impatience launched me to that library in hopes of meeting Charity Krans and having my suspicions confirmed, my hopes fulfilled.

I'd arrived late.

Charity was totally into whatever she was writing. Then I noticed Charity wasn't taking notes. She was sketching a horse. I loved Charity even more.

"Hey, Lorraine!"

For a moment I thought I was hearing voices and had suddenly become one of those people who heard their names called and got special messages from undiscovered planets and the inner workings of electric can openers, televisions, and satellite dishes. Then I heard it again, louder.

"Hey, Lorraine!"

It was Charity, and she had called my name. Oh my God! She knew my name and had called it. I was so excited I almost left the library because reality had already surpassed my expectations. But like a child, I believed there could be more to come. I racked my addled brain to think of the perfect, cool, mature response to this siren and said, "Hey."

"I hope you don't mind. Gerry told me your name. Thought I might see you again. My name is Charity Krans."

"I know. I mean I heard that was your name."

With boldness that did not match my stumbling words, only the courage in my imagination, and weakness in my knees, I took the remaining chair in the reference department and pulled it closer to Charity.

My eyes, like fingers on braille, moved slowly over Charity, the shelves of books and framed pictures of dead presidents fading to indistinct shadows. Charity's auburn hair; creamy pink skin; and round, hound-dog-brown eyes came clearly into focus. Her slender fingers used the pencil like a brush, the line sharp and thin here, dark and fat there, and then she tipped it over and shaded something so that the horse's muscles rippled and its mane wisped up from its neck.

Charity looked at me. We both wore jeans and white T-shirts that peeked out from crew neck sweaters. Charity's Sorel snow boots were empty, and her legs were knotted up beneath her. The sock closest to me was white with black words on it, nouns: earth, love, beauty, peace, solitude. I wanted to take Charity's foot in my hands and read her sock and have her turn onto her back and then stomach so that I didn't miss a word.

"I like your socks."

"Thanks, they're just regular socks, but I like to write on stuff. Do you want them?"

"Yes."

Charity slipped them off and handed them to me. The sock I couldn't see before was white with red verbs: walk, lie, sleep, run, touch. I held Charity Krans's socks and thought I might float away. I wanted to put them against my face like kisses.

"Are you sure your feet won't be cold?"

I was willing to put Charity's feet under my shirt and warm them against my stomach. I was willing to rub them between my hands and warm them. I hoped I wouldn't have to give the socks back.

"It's okay. My boots are warm enough. I drove over here. I'll be fine. I could drive you home later." She looked back at her sketch.

What we talked about was half blurred and half knitted into my DNA. I learned that Charity had turned nineteen and was finishing the last two courses of her sophomore year of college by correspondence, and the reason was a big convoluted story she wasn't ready to go into yet. I questioned her about everything she liked and loved, and counted only the things we had in common. God, we were virtually soul mates.

Charity confirmed what Gerry had told me. Charity Krans was Jolene Grind's older sister. Her last name was different because she'd changed it to her mother's maiden name once she was eighteen. While she was at it, she'd decided to take a new first name too.

"I'm surprised you haven't heard about me," Charity said. "Dad likes to use our family sins for his sermons. I've given him plenty of material."

"Jolene never told me about you. Did Jolene mention me?"

Charity leaned in. I could feel her breath on my face.

"Yeah, she told me about you, Lorraine Tyler. Jolene thought I might want to meet you since we may have the same condition. She's praying for me too."

God, it felt hot in that library.

She asked for my cell phone number, and I got mad at Momma and Dad all over again. "My folks won't let us have a cell phone, or internet, or college loans."

"Are they Luddites, you know those people who don't believe in technology?" she asked.

"No, they're just cheap and old-fashioned. They don't believe in anything above necessities, and Momma defines what we all need. We have a landline." I wrote our phone number on an index card and gave it to Charity.

The next step was obvious. When Charity drove me home, I invited her to come back the next day and see my mice. "One of the mommas just had babies. They look like a nest of pinkie fingers."

Charity said she'd come back to our farm the next morning at 10 a.m., and maybe we could take a walk, and she could sketch some trees and stuff. Charity dropped me off at home.

I wished I could call Jolene. It seemed like I should tell my best friend that I'd finally fallen in love, but again, I had to make my own path.

CHAPTER NINE
THE RENDEZVOUS

Charity said she had never dealt with animals other than cats and dogs and maybe a hamster, but she was excited to meet my animals. I had stoked the wood-burning stove in the barn so it was toasty for Charity to meet the beasts. Charity pulled off her mittens and knelt to greet the hounds. Pants and Sniff rubbed up against her and licked her hands and nosed her jeans. She held the mice, nuzzled the rabbits, and cooed at the chickens. I envied all of them.

Charity said just the right things: that the animals were cute and soft and that she understood why I wanted to take care of them. She asked if she could sketch them sometime. After Charity met the animals, I suggested that we take a hike in the woods, my most sacred place. I was confident about Charity meeting the animals, but didn't want to run into Momma, the real beast, just yet.

Charity grabbed her sketch pad and toolbox of pencils and paints from her truck. We walked along the driveway where it had been plowed. Then I veered off to the beaten-down path I had made on my walks in the woods. I held the middle strand of barbed-wire fence down with my boot and pulled the top strand up so that Charity could slip through. We weaved through naked oaks, maples, and aspens into the pasture west of the house. It had been a dry winter by Minnesota standards. The snow was not deep even off the trail. The snow crunched beneath our boots and our breaths hung like small clouds in front of our faces.

We crested a hill in the west pasture.

"That next farm belongs to Gerry Narrows, the librarian you met. The next farm after that is where Becky is going to live with Kenny Hollister. It's a stinky pig farm." I pointed to the south side of the farm.

"That side has more trees and that's Little Swan Lake. I'll show it to you in the spring. There's a road to get there, but we don't plow it in the winter. Dad uses the public access by the beach to put his fish house out."

We walked down to where the pasture woods sloped to the fence line. I brushed snow off a huge rock. We both got up on the rock and sat side by side. Charity removed her mittens, blew on her hands, and sketched. I could watch her do about anything for most of my lifetime. We sat quietly.

"Charity, can I ask you another more personal question?"

"Sure." She kept drawing. Her fingertips were smudged from where she blended the oil crayons, creating and blurring landscapes without sharp lines where a hill ended and trees and sky began. Her creation was a stark contrast to the white vista before us.

"Why'd you move here? What did you do?"

"Let's see. What did I do? Do you want my parents' version or the college's version?"

"I just want to know the truth."

"It's all true to somebody, Lorraine." Charity leaned in and let her shoulder nudge me, but I stayed on the rock as close to Charity as I could manage without getting in the way of her sketching.

"It didn't seem like you came home to Bend by your own choice. What happened?"

"I'm sorry. I don't mean to be flippant, but I have lived with so many stories and revisions of stories of what I did that I can't always remember what's true. No, that's not it." She looked at me. "I will always remember what I did. It's just that I learned that sometimes what really happened doesn't matter in the bigger picture."

"What happened matters to me."

Charity put one sketch aside and began another one in charcoal. I thought for a minute she wasn't going to tell me, but after a little while, she put her charcoal stick aside and put on her mittens and began her story.

Charity told how Jolene and her parents had moved to Bend when Charity had started her freshman year of college. She had spent the last two years completing her general education credits at a private school in St. Paul. Her parents had told her that if she kept her grades up and stayed out of trouble, they would foot the bill for her to finish a four-year art education degree.

"I bet my father thought I'd lose interest in more school, so he wouldn't have to keep his promise. He probably hoped I'd fall in love with some nice young man and get married and have a dozen babies." She removed her mittens again. I longed to reach out and hold her hands and warm them myself, but I sat on my own hands so I didn't do something premature and stupid. Charity sketched in birch trees, their white bark peeling and curling back. Some thorny bushes and sharp-bladed tall grasses poked through the snow cover in the foreground.

"I fell in love, with a woman. She was older and a part-time instructor named Kelly. I never told my parents. Mom would have cried and asked what she did wrong. She'd have scheduled me with a psychiatrist. It would have been worse if Dad found out. He'd insist on an exorcism."

Word had gotten back to the administration at the school that one of the teachers was in a sexual relationship with a student. The woman was only a couple of years older than Charity, but she was technically an adjunct faculty member. Charity's parents could have raised holy hell even though Charity was a legal adult. Charity told the school administrators that she wouldn't testify against the woman and said she wouldn't tell her minister father what had happened as long as the school didn't either. She'd made a deal that she would tell her dad she was kicked off campus for too much partying. The school administrator, who was probably very relieved, had gone along with the lie and told Charity she was not to contact the instructor again and vice versa.

Charity took some colored pencils from her tackle box and added shades of orange behind the trees, each value darker than the one before, and in no time what looked like a winter-sky–encompassed sunrise came into focus. Charity had transformed the tranquil winter scene into a raging fire that raced over the ground, through the trees, and poured toward the bushes.

"I had to leave Kelly, my friends, and everything. Now my parents watch me all the time like they think I'm some sort of alcoholic, and they don't understand that my heart is broken missing Kelly, not parties." Her eyes teared up. "I can't tell them. They'll think I'm broken. They won't get that I can't help that I love women. I didn't choose it like the way a person chooses which pop to drink or whether to write with a pen or pencil." Charity continued sketching.

"When did you know you were, you know?"

"Queer, odd, homosexual, lesbian? You have to learn to say the words, Lorraine."

"Well, when did you know you were lesbian?" I choked a bit on my own words.

"Looking back, I think my first inkling came when I was really young—maybe five or six. I loved my kindergarten teacher, Mrs. Anderson. I loved the way she looked, the way she smelled, the way she moved. I brought her dumb presents, my cookies from snack time. That was just the start. I had crush after crush on female teachers and women at church. I had no interest in boys, but I tried to be interested like my friends."

"I tried too," I said. "I even dated boys from my class. I didn't hate it exactly, but I didn't like it."

"Tell me about it. My dad brought home boys from whatever church he was leading, or boys he heard about when he was meeting with other pastors. I have been groped by so many so-called Christian boys and minister's sons that I threatened to run away if he didn't stop."

"Did he stop?"

"Are you kidding? My dad never gives up. He arranged dates for me right up until I moved into the dorm and he moved to Bend," she said. "Jolene even tried to get him to lay off."

"What did you do?"

"I tried to ignore him. Other times I made up lurid stories about having sex with every one of the boys he tried to set me up with."

"You loved Kelly?" I made myself say the name.

"Yep, I think I did. Too late now." Charity stopped drawing and smiled as she handed me her sketchbook and wrapped her arms around herself.

Orange, cadmium orange, raw sienna, and burnt sienna flames licked and lurched forward over the grasses in the sketch. Charity took the sketchbook back. With her left hand she grabbed vine charcoal sticks and brushed them and broke them onto the paper where the consuming fire released choking ivory and black smoke. Charity made the sky even angrier, and she covered the midsections of the trees with crimson and violet. The roots and trunks came up from the ground, but waded in a lake of fire.

I wanted to ask if Charity was really over Kelly, and where Kelly was. How could it be over? Were they still in love? But my throat stung and tightened from the sight of the sketch. Charity had made the fires of hell consume every living thing in their path. Was that what it felt like for her being away from Kelly? I took a deep breath and steeled myself. I found the nerve to ask Charity something.

"Would you go with me to my sister's wedding? I mean, I have to go because I'm in it, but would you come too?"

Charity gathered up her art supplies and moved closer to me. She wasn't teary anymore.

"Lorraine, are you asking me on a date?"

I could swear I saw more color coming to Charity's face, but maybe it was just the reflection of my blushing mug. There was no good reason to expect a college woman to have any interest in a high school senior like me, but something gave me reason to hope. Charity smiled and leaned into my shoulder. It was like a jolt of courage.

"Have you ever been to a small-town wedding?" I asked.

"No."

"Well after the serious stuff at the church, things loosen up. There's a reception-like dinner at the dance hall. They hold the dinner there for a couple reasons. For one thing, most people get pretty drunk because there's an open bar the first two hours. People drink fast when the booze is free. With all that drinking the parents don't want folks driving to a new place for the dance. They all hope that the dancing afterward and drinks no longer being free will sober people up in time to drive home. Another thing, the men would rather drink than dance, so women dance with women." I looked at Charity to see if she caught my drift. Charity was way ahead of me. She dropped her sketchbook and sprang off the rock.

"Lorraine, are you saying a gal could hold another gal like this?" Charity grabbed me around my back with her right arm, took my right hand into her left hand, and pulled me into a standing position.

You couldn't have slipped frog's hair in the space between our bodies. I had never been held by another woman except for brief hugs of congratulations by my parents, friends, and church folks. This was not the same. Electricity shot through my body.

"Could a gal hold another gal this close?" Charity pressed against me. Our faces were only inches apart.

"Yes, and maybe a couple of gals could keep dancing even after the other dancers went home," I said before I twirled Charity.

"Well, we are two gals who shouldn't miss that opportunity." Charity spun me around again and looked at me with narrowed eyes like she was going to say something, or maybe even kiss me. Then she let me go. "Maybe being exiled to Bend isn't so bad after all."

CHAPTER TEN
A WEDDING IN BEND

B ecky married Kenny Hollister on the second Saturday in January. It was still five months before we would graduate from high school and turn eighteen, and six months before she was due to deliver a baby. She had registered for gifts at the Mills Fleet Farm, the same place Kenny bought supplies for his hogs. It didn't matter that her grades were the highest in our class, she couldn't win the scholarship because she was pregnant. I had hoped Becky would just postpone her college enrollment until she had the money, but Becky canceled it entirely, and seemingly without regret.

I was Becky's reluctant maid of honor, and flanked her with three other girls in pink dresses that could have been seen from outer space and had no practical purpose beyond that little jaunt down the aisle for Becky. Wearing the long-sleeved, pink frilly dress; the pink-dyed shoes; the panty hose; and having my curls pinned back with bobby pins and plastered with hairspray didn't chafe me as much as I had imagined. I was preoccupied with love and lust. I was about to have my first real date with Charity.

Getting through the ceremony and pictures was a trial. I swore I could feel Charity's eyes on me from where Charity and Jolene sat as spectators. To make matters worse, Kenny's cousin, Frank Hollister, was my escort. Frank was best man in the wedding sense and he had a body right off the cover of *Sports Illustrated*, but his brawn and chiseled features were wasted on me. He smelled nice, but it irked me that he didn't have the sense to keep his hands off me. Finally, after two warnings and one sharp blow to his instep, Frank stopped touching me.

Becky's long, layered white gown bulged at the waist, but still created a sparkly universe around her. Her veil gave no clue that behind its lace, and her glowing face, was a mind that had scored the highest marks anybody in Bend had ever gotten in the college-preparation tests. Her high scores didn't mean anything. She'd buckled under pressure from Momma, the school superintendent, and Pastor Grind to finish her school year at home, like she was somehow contagious. Kenny had quit already.

For the wedding, Momma wore her new blue dress and had a perm. Dad wore his one and only suit—a black specimen with thin lapels that I had only ever seen in funeral pictures and slouching on a metal hanger in the hall closet. He'd had a haircut and a close shave. He looked Paul Newman handsome. His skin smelled like Old Spice cologne, and his breath was minty at the wedding and smelled like Grain Belt Beer at the reception.

Becky and Kenny were hitched without a hitch. Pictures didn't take very long because of a lack of relatives. Kenny's folks were twenty years older than Momma and Dad, and they hadn't come to the wedding. Word was that Mr. Hollister was too sick and senile for Mrs. Hollister to leave him at home, and nobody'd volunteered to stay with him. Kenny's two older sisters came from out of town, but left immediately after the ceremony like they were wanted criminals.

The reception dragged on and on. Appetite eluded me. I was too nervous in anticipation of dancing with Charity at the wedding dance. I passed up the deviled eggs, potato salad, sliced turkey and ham on white buns, and five shades of Jell-O. The cake, three tiers of white pound cake and lard-based frosting, didn't tempt me at all. I nibbled dove- and rose-shaped mints to keep my breath fresh.

Kenny's buddies clinked their glasses repeatedly so that the newlyweds had to kiss. Considering that Becky was already three months pregnant, I didn't understand the titillation of making them kiss each other.

Bend wedding traditions dictated that the dance immediately followed the reception. Becky and Kenny would have rather had a DJ, but Momma and Dad were paying. The band was five white men in their sixties who looked like they would have rather been playing the hundred waltzes and four thousand polkas they knew than the dozen rock songs that were all older than me. They played trumpet, tuba, drums, accordion, keyboard, and occasionally molested an electric guitar.

I loved it. I sat with Charity and Jolene, where a constant string of blurry-eyed boys paraded over and asked Jolene to dance. Older boys and young men sniffed around Charity and asked her to dance, but she turned them all down. Charity only danced with me.

I held Charity in my arms and danced the "Beer Barrel Polka," the "Too Fat Polka," and "Hoop-Dee-Doo." I cursed the few rock songs they played because it meant I had to let Charity go. I wasn't brave enough to insist we dance to the couple of slow songs the band played. I wondered if what I was feeling was what Becky felt as she twirled with Kenny. I couldn't know for certain, but I doubted my feeling that good hurt anybody else.

When the dance ended, Charity and I lingered in a booth. I people-watched and narrated the scene for Charity. The band members packed up, the men red-faced and spent. Becky massaged her lower back, tired after a long day of celebration with another person inside her. Kenny high-fived with everybody and hugged his drunken school buddies. Twitch held court at the bar, surrounded by a mixture of married and unmarried women giving audience to his stories and jokes. He ran his own little rodeo in his sport coat, dressy cowboy boots, and hat.

"Just look at Twitch, Charity. I don't know what it is about him." I leaned in to whisper. "Those women look ready to lasso him, tie him up like a calf, but take him home and use him like a bull."

From the middle of the dance floor, Dad jumped up and down while he laughed and pulled streamers loose from the rafters. Momma positioned herself at the dance hall door and thanked each person for coming, telling them to drive home safely in a tone that sounded more like an order than a good wish. She probably eyed people to make certain they hadn't stolen any glasses or plates.

Pastor Grind made an appearance, didn't dance, and stopped at our table twice, I suppose to make certain Charity wasn't drinking. Little did he know what was really transpiring at our table.

I flirted mercilessly with Charity—wrote silly love poems for her on bar napkins, told her how much I liked dancing with her, and I was just about to ask Charity to drive me home when Momma appeared and declared that I would need to drive the station wagon home. Dad had drunk his usual couple of beers and Momma wouldn't let him drive.

"Can't you drive him home?"

"I'm just too tired, dear," Momma said.

"Wait, I can't. I'm not allowed to drive the station wagon until I'm twenty-six." I thought I had found a loophole that appealed to Momma's zeal for rules and consequences. "You said so yourself."

Nothing worked. Momma suspended my driving suspension for that trip home. I waved a weak good-bye to Charity. I was left to wonder if I would have been kissed on my first real date.

CHAPTER ELEVEN
THE BLESSING

Winter melted into spring. Lo and behold, in early May it was announced that I had won the McGerber scholarship. It was what I wanted, but I was still mad as hell. I had wanted to beat Becky fair and square over grades, not over somebody else's morals and idea of what God expects. Becky had the better grades, but she couldn't have the scholarship because she got pregnant while still in high school. I was enraged on Becky's behalf and also scared that the same beast with morality claws could be coming for me next.

It just all felt weird. I had a room to myself because Becky lived with Kenny and completed her schoolwork from there, but I couldn't sleep in there anymore. I tossed and turned and said things waiting for Becky to yell something at me, but then I remembered she wasn't in the upper bunk. I visited Becky and listened to the new bride and expectant mother talk about God's hand fluttering in her womb and Biblical names for the baby. I was kind of excited about being an aunt, but not if I had to call the kid Hezekiah or something weird.

I studied, and worked at the diner and with Twitch. I saw Charity whenever I could, which made me both terribly excited and scared out of my wits. She was older than me, she'd already had a girlfriend before that she'd loved, so why would she ever care about a seventeen-year-old nobody? I met her at the library. We took walks. I dreamed of what it would be like to kiss her, but I didn't try anything and I didn't sit still enough for her to kiss me even if she wanted to. I insulated my heart to protect against breakage.

When graduation day finally arrived, Becky and Kenny came to the ceremony, where classmates clustered around them and made polite conversation even though I'd heard some of the same people make snide remarks behind their backs. Becky didn't blink. She held her head up above her ripe belly and greeted and God-blessed all those two-faced well-wishers. I wished I could punch each one of them for her, but I was proud that she was a better scholar and a better person than me.

Both Becky and I finished high school, but only I sang a sappy song with other members of the Bend senior choir. Only I was allowed to wear a cap and gown and be on the stage with the rest of the senior class. I accepted my diploma but refused to shake the superintendent's hand, because he was part of the stubbornness and shame that left Becky in the bleacher seats.

After I collected my awards, I was expected to make the type of speech that most valedictorians of small high schools make. I was supposed to talk about new beginnings for graduates and how our parents, teachers, churches, and towns were the foundations upon which we would build our strong characters. I spoke very briefly and choked back tears.

"I thank my dad and momma for raising me on the most beautiful land in the world. I thank Dr. Benjamin Twitchell for teaching me about animals and showing me the job I want for my whole life. I thank my sister, Becky, for showing me how to study. I wish all my classmates and every person here all the things I wish for myself. I wish you the opportunity to go to college if you want. I wish you the opportunity to have the job that makes you happy. I wish you the opportunity to fall in love and have your parents, church, school, and friends be happy for you. Thank you for your attention and good luck."

The applause was slow and spotty. I recognized some hoots and hollers from Dad and Twitch.

As salutatorian, Jolene Grind spoke next. She talked about God's blessings, God's warnings, and I thought she might have mentioned God's recipe for good barbecue.

Momma and Dad put together a graduation party for Becky and me at the farm. I bolted early. I couldn't stand one more congratulations from somebody when my momma hadn't yet said a word about me winning the scholarship. She'd had less than a month to get used to the idea that her heathen daughter was a scholarship winner, but still, she could be happy for me if for no other reason than I'd be out of the house without costing her any money.

I ate potato salad, Jell-O, sloppy joes, and ham and cheese sandwiches until I thought I'd blow up. I stayed the longest at Jolene's house, where I flirted with Charity and talked with Jolene. That night at Grind's house, I learned officially who'd told Grind about Becky and Kenny having sex. It was Jolene.

"You should've won that scholarship from the start. You're the better student and the better person." Jolene hugged me. "I'm sorry it took me squealing to get it done. I'm not exactly proud of that, but it was all I could think of doing. You need to have a chance to get away from Bend."

"You're a good friend, Jolene." I didn't tell her that I felt really crappy about winning that scholarship right then.

"Your momma and dad must be pretty proud of you." Jolene looked at me.

"Dad hugged me. He cried a little too. Momma hasn't said anything yet. I think she's pretty disappointed Becky didn't get it. Go figure. Becky doesn't even want to go to college anymore. She wants to have babies and live on a pig farm with Kenny."

I had applied and been accepted for school at a four-year state college two hours north without knowing if I had the money to pay for it. Now, technically, I had the money to pay for it if I could live in the dorm, but I had lost in the lottery drawing for housing. I couldn't live in the dorm and the money I had wasn't enough to pay for living off campus. It seemed like there was always something keeping one or both of my legs in a trap in Bend.

Gerry helped me call the college and delay my entrance until spring of the next year, when there would likely be a spot open in the dorm. That setback might have put me in a total tailspin if it weren't for my thoughts of having a niece or nephew in July. I planned to teach that child every bad behavior they could grasp. That way Becky wouldn't miss me so much. Plus, as much as I wasn't sure I'd ever get the courage to do it, I wanted to kiss Charity before I left for college.

Graduation festivities trickled over into June and stopped. Becky and I turned eighteen that month, but had separate birthday parties. I celebrated by riding from town-to-town with Charity and Jolene. It was our first annual birthday pie tour. We sampled pies at every restaurant we found, played miniature golf in St. Wendell, and went swimming at the beach at Little Swan Lake. The three of us stayed at the beach long into the night, huddled around a raging bonfire we'd made with fallen tree branches. We sang camp songs and hymns we knew from church and top forties along with Charity's CD player. We talked about our dreams. I censored my answers some for Jolene's sake and comfort.

CHAPTER TWELVE
IMMERSION

I had already been somewhat of a fixture at the Grind place since Jolene and I'd become friends, but after Charity moved into what was at first her art studio above the garage and with some convincing became her studio apartment above the garage, I started manufacturing reasons to go there. I brought eggs. I brought the whole chicken when we were butchering. I livetrapped animals Charity might enjoy seeing or sketching. I found landscapes and lake scenes I thought Charity just had to paint. I wrote corny sayings and thinly veiled love poems for Charity to use on future clothing-writing projects.

True to her word, Jolene hadn't told anyone about me kissing her cheek. If it bugged her that Charity and I spent time together, she didn't say anything about it. Pastor Grind ignored all three of us. We became a threesome in crime when we rescued the ornaments Momma had taken from Dad's lawn display and thrown in the dumpster by the gas station. We loaded the bobbles into Charity's truck and hid them in one of Grind's outbuildings until another night when Charity and I placed them back in the yard.

I'd like to think it was me, or maybe it was living in Bend, that had been surprisingly inspirational for Charity's painting and drawing. She made a boatload of paintings and drawings. She seemed to gain confidence. She said she wanted to prove she could work in any medium, including pottery, when she applied for art school in St. Paul, and was determined to use her time in Bend to build a portfolio. It was Charity's desire to throw pots that ended up bringing my dad and her together. He offered to help her rig up a pottery wheel.

It was a summer scorcher when Dad let me drive us over to the Grind place in his truck. Jolene, Charity, and I watched as Dad attached an electric motor to a twirling stool. Before very long, he was on the ground wiring a switch so Charity could control the speed of the wheel with a foot pedal. While he was down on his back, Pastor and Mrs. Grind came out of their house. Mrs. Grind waved to the group and went to the car. Pastor Grind crossed the lawn like he owned the place—which he did. Then he stood over Dad.

"Good thing you're here, Joseph. My eight years of college and seminary didn't equip me for work like this."

"No. Work like this is best left to the uneducated. I see you still got an empty cement slab. I thought you wanted another garage. Are you growing one?"

"Give my best to Peggy, Joseph." Grind joined his wife in the car and drove off.

"Can I get you a pop or some lemonade, Mr. Tyler?" Jolene asked.

"I don't suppose you have any beer," he said.

Jolene didn't answer, only smiled.

"No. I don't suppose you do. I'm fine Jolene. Thanks." He got up and dusted off his pants. "I've got some good bricks in the back of the truck. Where should we put your kiln?"

Charity gave him a look, something between simple gratitude and worshipful adoration. I coveted the response.

"Let's put it where Dad's been trying to grow a garage," Charity said. After Dad finished the kiln, Charity asked him if he minded if she brought me home a little bit later.

"It's okay with me." Dad's face reddened as Charity hugged him quick. "Well, yeah, I better get home and see what job Peggy has for me."

Jolene said she was going to drive to Will's Diner and order a bowl of ice cream the size of her head, or the size of my head; she was really hungry. Since Jolene didn't invite us along, Charity and I were alone.

"Enough of this. You look really hot, Lorraine," Charity said.

Crap. I almost wet my pants. *She thinks I'm really hot.*

"I have a job for us. We're going to wash my truck."

While Charity got the hose and buckets, I pulled my tank top loose from my jeans. I wondered if my breasts were smaller than average. I tried to herd my hair back under my cap, but then gave up.

"What do you think of Bend now that you've been here awhile?" That question veiled my true wonderment. I was too afraid to ask how long Charity planned to stay.

Charity took her time answering. She soaped most of the front panel of her truck before she spoke. "Well, this town has a ferocious appetite for hardware and God."

"What do you mean?"

"Do the math. There are only two grocery stores, two gas stations, two cafés, two barber shops, one lumberyard, one school, one bank, one feed store, a post office, one library, one senior center, one bar, one creamery, one butcher shop, one ceramics shop, but there are three hardware stores and three churches. There are only four hundred people who live here. Why would you need three hardware stores and three churches?"

"Well, first of all, I must defend our hunger for hardware. Those hardware stores are all different and necessary in their own way." While I formulated the lie that I hoped would sound like an amusing story, I rinsed my sponge in the bucket.

Before I could elaborate, Charity interrupted.

"But what about the churches? Why do you need three churches? I'm sure my dad would argue that the one he runs is sufficient for everyone."

"I'd have an easier time explaining the hardware store surplus, but I suppose three churches aren't much to try to catch four hundred souls. I don't know that the churches are that much different from each other. Although, I have to admit I admire the Catholics. They can go to mass at 5 p.m. on Saturday afternoon, go about their business or pleasure Saturday night, and sleep in on Sunday. Genius."

"I think people feel more comfortable thinking there are big differences between churches. My God's bigger than your God, God's on my side sort of thing."

I didn't say it, but I felt pretty certain that none of the churches in Bend would say God was on my side.

Once the truck was washed and rinsed, I flopped on the nearest stretch of grass we hadn't soaked. Charity piled the rags and sponges in the buckets and dragged the hose to the side of the garage and coiled it below the spigot. A hissing I hadn't noticed until it was gone cleared my ears when Charity turned off the water. She flopped down on the grass next to me.

I watched the clouds awhile. I turned to Charity. "Do you still believe in God?"

"Yeah, don't you?"

"I want to. I want to believe all the stories about Jesus helping the poor and sick. I want to believe that I'll never die. Then, I don't know. I go to church and . . ." I waited a beat and then I said it. "And I'm a queer. The church says God doesn't want me."

Charity didn't answer anything right away, and I thought about taking the question back somehow so that Charity would never hear my dumb response. Charity propped her head on her bent arm and touched the top of my shoulder.

"You see the way this part of your arm curves here and dips down where more muscle begins? God made that. And look here." She turned my arm over so that it lay on the ground palm up, and she grazed her fingers along my inner arm from elbow to wrist. "This skin here couldn't possibly be any smoother. God did that." She traced my fingers, gliding her own up and down and between each one. "You see how sensitive and precise our hands can be? That's God's work."

Pain could radiate through the body. A headache could express itself down a person's neck and back. I knew all that, but I didn't know pleasure could land on and invade so much territory. I felt Charity's hand on mine throughout my whole body, like my nerves were gossiping to each other and sending up flares saying, *Touch me next.*

"God created everything. Come closer," she said. I mirrored her position and tried to remember to breathe and then to breathe slower.

"Shut your eyes, Raine."

That was the first time she called me that. Raine. I didn't want to be called anything else ever again. Charity moved closer to my face. Her breath and words brushed my lips at the same time as she stroked my cheek. Her thumb passed below my eyelids.

"This cheekbone, God made it so that your smile would have a place to stop. And your lips, God made those too—a gift for you to share. I'll show you."

Then, in daylight, on Pastor Grind's front lawn, Charity Krans kissed me. The kiss was light at first, and then she kissed me more insistently. I leaned into her kiss like I had always known her mouth. And when she let me go, after lingering a moment with my lower lip between her lips, Charity said, "I believe in creator God who made us all and wants us to live and love with fullness and tenderness."

Oh Lord, I was suddenly a believer! Sprinkle me or dip me in the river. Hell, I was ready to be a missionary to the masses.

Charity sprang up, grabbed the sponges and buckets, and disappeared into the garage. Was this what had made Becky give up college? Keep me stupid and underemployed. I would live on love.

There was a paralysis in my legs and my pulse thumped enthusiastically in a few other spots. I didn't know whether to build a monument on that square of lawn, but I knew I wanted Charity to come right back and kiss me again and not stop until—until when? I couldn't think of any good reason to stop. Why had we stopped? It was that question that made me haul my numb butt off the ground. Before I reached the garage, Charity was out again, pulling the garage door down. Her keys were between her lips. I envied those keys.

"Well, I better get you home before your momma comes looking for you. Besides, I still want to try my potter's wheel."

"We just kissed right? I didn't fall on my head. It really happened?" I got in Charity's truck. I touched my lips with my fingertips and vowed never to wash them again in case Charity's lips never touched me again.

"Yeah. It was real Lorraine. You're a good kisser. Now, put on your seat belt so you don't damage those lips by crashing against the dashboard if I stop to avoid a squirrel or something."

"Charity, I'm just so happy, and I don't know."

"It's okay. Let it be."

Not one to let a subject go, but too scared to be very direct, I changed the subject.

"Dad always says it was love at first sight when he met my momma. I can't imagine that. I think she held him captive for a few years until he got used to her."

"How could she keep him if he didn't want to be there?"

"Strong ropes. Oh, and my momma is a good cook."

"So she tied him up and won him over with meat loaf?"

"Say what you want about my momma, but tread careful when you talk about her meat loaf."

Charity laughed, but worried the topic more. "Do you really think your momma had to conquer your dad?"

"More like wore him down. You got to understand, my dad grew up poor. Food is greater than God to him. I bet he'd tell you himself that he's never seen God, but that hasn't hurt as much as the days when he and his ma, dad, and five brothers didn't see food. He learned to trap, hunt, and fish because he liked to eat."

I don't remember ever going on about my parents' history, let alone their love affair, but I couldn't stop myself from blabbing. "The lakes and woods around here were his grocery store. He told me his ma taught him to season flour, coat the fish, and fry them in a cast iron skillet—part cooking utensil, part weapon. Bacon grease flavored them and kept them from sticking. The heat of the cook stove was mildly regulated, only two settings, out and hell. He never took for granted the efforts it took to secure and prepare food. He told me he spit on his fish as they cooked so his brothers didn't steal them from him.

"Then he met Momma, and she tamed him and eroded his resistance with marbled beef roasted in a nest of carrots, new potatoes, and whole pearl onions. When he tasted her gravy he was done for. He sopped it up with those crusty molasses buns she makes, and he became a man with severe back trouble. He had no spine to leave."

"You make me hungry, Lorraine." Charity put her hand just above me knee.

"I was thinking the same thing about you."

"Well, I think you and your dad are both romantics. I think he and your momma have always loved each other. They have you and your sister. So they must have sex together."

"We don't know that for certain. We aren't identical twins. Did I mention I'm four minutes older than Becky? Besides, Becky is odd looking—she could be something spawned some other way. You know my momma never mentions scarring, and to meet Becky you got to believe she came out clawing and kicking."

"What about you? Did you come out of your momma clawing and kicking?" She slid her hand higher on my leg.

Gulp. "Nope, I think my dad birthed me, or maybe he made me from wood, or tamed a squirrel until it turned into me, and that's why I love it so much in the woods. I was a squirrel."

"You're a squirrel all right. That much I believe." Charity took her hand off my leg and put it back on that undeserving, unappreciative steering wheel. "So your momma tamed your dad and your dad tamed you and your sister sprouted like fungus? Is that what you're saying?"

"Yep, I can live with that explanation."

CHAPTER THIRTEEN
THE BIRTH

By the time July dawned, Becky and I were both ensconced in our assigned places. I was living with Momma and Dad, and Becky had moved into a preowned, double-wide trailer house on the Hollister farm. From their kitchen window, I could see the sheds Kenny and his dad used to house the sows while the pigs were about to drop a litter. Like the pigs, Becky would farrow in a tin house.

While Becky became double-wide herself and played house with her new husband, I worked with Twitch a little, but mostly at the diner with Momma. Becky and I had learned to walk by climbing the same red Naugahyde booths and stools. Dad swore our first words were, "Order up!" Momma said that was a lie. That our first words were, "Don't forget to tip your waitress!"

It wasn't a big stretch for me to start working there full-time after working there part-time every summer since I turned fifteen. Plus, I wasn't doing it because I lost the scholarship. I had won the scholarship, and earning extra money by working at the diner was my choice mostly. I'd have rather been working with Twitch, but Momma said scholarship or not, I would make more money at the diner. I didn't believe in Momma's math abilities, but I had every confidence in Momma's boxing skills. So, I didn't argue the point.

The tedium was broken by visits from Charity, who flirted mercilessly with me even when Jolene was along. Momma noticed Charity's comings and goings, but seemed pleased.

"I'm glad you're spending time with those girls. I hope some of their good sense rubs off on you, Lorraine. You know, Allister and I were close friends when we were in high school together in Clearmont. He had quite an influence on me."

Being "close" was an understatement when I thought about Charity. The venue didn't matter: Charity and I made out in Charity's truck, the woods, the beach, and a half dozen other private spots. We kissed a lot, but never enough in my mind. I didn't ask for more than that because I wasn't quite sure what was next. I only knew my body felt like it couldn't be physically close enough to Charity. It was like I wanted to crawl inside the girl and roll around. There was no mention of Charity's former girlfriend, Kelly.

When I wasn't with Charity I was thinking about her. I was doing just that when the phone rang early on a Saturday. I answered.

"It's coming out, it's coming out," somebody yelled. The voice sounded familiar, but I gave the screeching contraption to Dad.

Dad interpreted the call, hung up, and told me that Becky was in labor.

While Momma packed a lunch, extra bath towels, and a thermos of coffee, I called Twitch and waited outside for him to pick me up. Apparently, Momma made her own call and a midwife named Dorcas got to Becky and Kenny's trailer before us.

"I've come to guide Becky's baby into the world," Twitch said, as he made his entrance to the trailer in front of me. He smiled at Momma and attempted to follow the whining and crying sounds to the back bedroom.

"Becky doesn't need your fool face in her personal business," Momma said. "Dorcas is here, and she'll deliver the baby. You can stand by and if there's complications, I'll need you to rush her to a proper hospital."

I imagined this Dorcas having set up a CD player with soothing music and sitting with a beatific smile as she massaged Becky's lower back. I had to use my imagination because Momma wouldn't let me near Becky either.

Momma waltzed past Twitch after she pointed us to the living room where Dad and Kenny waited. We greeted each other and sat like we were in the dentist's lobby, but the magazines were worse.

The afternoon wore on, and I wished I'd brought a book, a very long book. Dad remained cheerful as he paged through *Hog Breeding Today*, and Twitch quizzed me on castrating pigs. I wanted to tell Twitch we were at least nine months too slow on practicing that skill. I stared at Kenny. Our conversation moved him. He went into the kitchen, pacing back and forth while he ate a bologna and mayonnaise sandwich. He didn't offer us anything.

Becky screamed, "Get that goddamned giraffe out of here!"

Dad, Twitch, and I looked at each other, smiling and laughing because we all knew that was really silly. Newborn giraffes measured six feet long.

When the squeals changed tone and Momma started praising God very loudly and yelling, "It's a boy, it's a boy," Kenny made for the bedroom. Dad, Twitch, and I squeezed into the hallway outside the bedroom door and listened. I heard a baby gurgle and cry. Becky'd had a baby boy.

Wordlessly, I attempted a border crossing. Twitch and Dad followed me. We peeked into the room and edged closer. Becky looked flushed, exhausted, and euphoric. Kenny sat beside her on the bed and stroked her hair. The baby was lying on Becky's chest and belly like a little otter. Our collective "Ahhh!" caught Momma's attention, and she quickly herded us back to the neutral zone.

"Becky and Kenny need time with the baby to themselves," she said, but she made no move to leave herself. Momma even shooed the midwife out the door with rushed thanks.

Dorcas, Twitch, Dad, and I stood in the yard outside the trailer and looked at each other like we'd all been mugged. We had endured the wait, the heat of the trailer, the screaming, and had nothing to show for the trouble.

"Schafer's cow is calving today—could be twins," Twitch said, offering me a fair substitute. "You want to come with me and help me pull 'em out? Unless you have dishes to wash or cookies to bake at the diner? I wouldn't want to interrupt your wife training."

He made the same offer to Dorcas and Dad, but only I followed him to his Jeep.

As he buckled his seat belt Twitch said, "I hope to hell the momma takes to both of them this time."

"What do you mean?"

"Well, sometimes the momma only takes to one calf. I suppose she wasn't expecting two mouths to feed. Anyway, she sometimes will only feed one of the twins."

"So even cows play favorites?" I said. "What do you do if some big old cow only likes one of her calves?"

"Two calves feeding take a toll on the cow's body. We are still just talking about cows, right?"

"Yeah, I'll let my annoyance with Momma rest for now. Let's talk cows."

"Good. Cows I understand. As you know, cows are pregnant for nine months and only have one calf a year. Once in a blue moon, they have twins."

"What will you do if the momma won't take to both babies?"

"At least if this cow has twins, we're going to know about both of them," Twitch said. "Jeff put the cow in the barn. That gives us a better chance than if she was out in the pasture and abandoned one. Today, we'll deliver them if she's ready, and we'll watch to see if she accepts both. If not, for a few days we'll try to convince her—keep her in the pen with both. Maybe we'll even let Schafer's cattle dog get after the rejected baby. That calf starts bawling and there aren't many cows that won't save their baby from something trying to kill it."

"That's it," I said. "Maybe you could find some wild dog to chase after me in front of Momma."

"I thought we were talking about cows."

"Sorry. Aren't you worried the dog might hurt the calf?"

"No, that dog—she'd juggle oranges for you if you asked. Worst comes to worst, we'll bottle-feed the baby she can't accept."

Only a few of the family's twelve children were in the yard when we arrived at the Schafer place. Jeff soothed a restless Jersey cow in a bedded calving pen in the barn. The caramel-colored beast was fitful, up one minute and on her side a few minutes later.

Twitch smiled at me. "Delivering healthy calves is like good comedy. It's all about timing. Help too early and you can hurt the cow and the calf. Help too late and you can hurt the cow and the calf." Twitch learned the cow had been edgy a good three hours. It wasn't but a few minutes before the cow was down on her side again, but this time she strained as she reacted to the contractions. Her tongue swabbed her nose and lips. Then, she gave a better effort at pushing.

It wasn't long before a purplish blue, egg-shaped thing protruded from her vulva. The cow was about to deliver her water bag.

"I hope we can do this without Dorcas and her instrumental music." I tried to look serious.

"Very funny," Twitch said. "I'll check the position of the calf. She's straining, but not pushing continually yet." He put on shoulder-length filmy gloves and lubed his hands and arm. He put his right hand inside the cow by the water bag.

"Yep, she's in place—two feet and a nose." Twitch smiled.

The calf had slid into the birth canal, and it was positioned right for delivery. The cow would probably do the whole thing herself with less screaming than I'd heard from Becky. But if there was trouble and the labor took too long, Twitch and I would help the cow so that we didn't risk oxygen deprivation for the calf.

"The feet and head are forward like the little sucker is ready to dive out into the world." Twitch kept the glove on and watched.

The cow took breaks between pushing, but then picked up the pace. Once the nose and toes presented enough, Twitch checked the calf's tongue. It was pink and the calf pulled it back when Twitch pinched it.

"No distress."

It took another hour for the calf to come fully into the world. Twitch checked the cow and determined he'd been wrong. There was only one calf. The momma cow wouldn't have to divide her affections. I petted the calf's wet head and suggested Jeff name her Lucky.

CHAPTER FOURTEEN
THE SON

The next day Momma sounded the all clear, and I went to see the baby. He was tucked in the crook of Becky's arm as she talked to him. Her voice didn't have the shrill weed whacker tone she usually used with me. Becky whispered. I scanned the air around Becky's head for bubbles or clouds rising from Becky's lips. The baby studied Becky's face like he remembered her from somewhere else, but couldn't place her. His birdie hands came up to Becky's nose. She kissed his hands, face, and head.

Becky looked up at me. "Come in here, Lorraine. Come see what love has made."

That sort of sentiment, paired with my memories of Becky and Kenny having sex on the concession stand floor, almost sent me in the opposite direction, but something about the way Becky held that thing and the different person Becky seemed to be, loving that pink grub, made me want to see it and examine Becky more closely. Maybe Becky's meanness had festered in her uterus all along and splashed out with the placenta.

"Pull that chair over close so you can see Kenny Jr. It is really the Lord Jesus, savior of the world," Becky whispered. "But don't tell anyone just yet."

"Yeah, I'll keep that part under my hat." I giggled, but squelched it when I saw that Becky wasn't laughing.

"I'll let you hold him once your hands warm up."

It was July. My hands weren't cold from weather, but they were chilled from nerves. I guessed anybody's hands would be too cold for holding a baby, especially if that baby was the son of God. I blew on my hands, rubbed them on my jeans, and finally, sat on them while I leaned forward to see the face that absorbed Becky's attention.

The little guy was cute in his own baby way, everything so miniaturized and with a layer of blond fuzz all over the parts of him I could see. His head had dents and bulges from his journey, but the hair there was longer and curled up in places like lake waves caught still.

"Are you ready?" Becky asked. "Is my Little Man ready to meet his auntie?"

Just to be sure, I touched my hand against Becky's arm to see if she thought I was warm enough. Becky nodded slightly, skootched over on the bed, and lowered Kenny Jr. into my arms.

"That's Kenneth Allan Hollister Jr., but I've been calling him Little Man." She smiled at Little Man and then at me.

He was weightless, but I held him like he might be nitroglycerin and ready to blow. Then he looked at me, and he seemed more like a puppy than an explosive. I nestled him against my chest and petted his fingers, cheeks, and eyebrows with my index finger.

"Little Man. I love you."

Becky smiled at me and mouthed the words herself. Then she said, "Isn't he beautiful?"

"Yeah, Becky. He's even cuter than a baby bunny." I meant it. I was right there with Becky and Little Man. There wasn't anywhere else I wanted to be. I marveled that I had fallen in love at first sight twice in the same year, first with Charity and then with Little Man.

"You better make something of that scholarship, I swear, Lorraine." Becky shook her finger at me.

"Becky, you don't swear." I couldn't remember the last time I had joked with Becky. "You might not believe it, but I'm really sorry you missed out on the scholarship." I kept my eyes fixed on Little Man, but at least half my heart reached toward Becky.

"Thanks for the sentiment, Lorraine. I have something better than any grades or scholarship right here. God has spoken to me, Lorraine. I am the mother of the new Jesus. Can you believe it?" Becky nodded towards Little Man. "The blessings just keep coming. Someday you'll understand, Lorraine. Someday, when you love somebody."

Becky looked up and reached for Little Man. Just above her elbow on both arms were bruises like the ones Kenny had given me the day he grabbed me hard. Before I could ask her what the hell happened, Kenny Sr. walked into the room and Becky got all riled up.

"Give him back to me now, Lorraine," she said. "I don't want him getting any of your queer germs."

I transferred Little Man back to Becky. Immediately, Becky whipped out a breast and the baby latched on like a snapping turtle. Kenny looked at me like I was seeing something too private for my eyes. Hell, I wanted to say I'd seen more of Becky every day than what she revealed breast-feeding and I'd seen all his parts too. Neither were that impressive to me. Kenny glared at me. I needed no other reason to get out of there.

When Momma, Dad, and I weren't working, we waited for Becky and Kenny to bring Little Man over. It was like we shared a toy with Becky, and we needed to sit close together in order to both touch it and watch it work. If Becky took too long to come to the farm, we piled in the station wagon and went over to Becky and Kenny's trailer.

"Lorraine, do us a big favor and take our picture." Kenny stumbled over himself as he captured their new life on film. It amazed me that the kid wasn't blinded by all the flashes from that camera, but every movement and smile seemed to require a permanent record. That didn't shock me, but it about floored me that Kenny was nice to me and Becky didn't act all self-righteous like I might give the baby queer germs or HIV.

"You hold him now and sit with Becky there on the couch, and I'll take your picture," Kenny said. "Let me get two pictures so you have one for yourself." Our hips touched, and Becky put her head on my shoulder. Together, we cradled Little Man with a pride I couldn't imagine we'd share for anything else.

All the fighting stopped. I didn't fight with Becky. Momma didn't fight with Dad. Momma and Dad were probably glad for the reprieve. It gave them energy to do other things. Dad went fishing with Twitch. A competitive game player, Momma looked for someone to beat.

She could play gin, pinochle, Monopoly, poker, blackjack, and whist, but her favorite game was Scrabble.

Gerry Narrows had never been invited to our house even though Momma and Gerry grew up in the same hometown and she was our neighbor. Once Becky had the baby, Gerry stopped by the trailer to see her and the baby weekly. She usually brought something new she'd knit for the baby. The stitch was so tight that the outfits were like chain mail armor. On one such visit, Becky sent Gerry to our house to see the baby. Momma was prepared. The baby was the bait and that Scrabble board on the kitchen table was the trap. Gerry was caught as soon as she saw it.

I suppose Gerry expected to win. She'd been a school teacher prior to getting a doctoral degree in library science, she was a crossword puzzle whiz, and my momma had never attended college. Logic be damned, Momma beat Gerry soundly two straight games.

Having a son had softened Becky, and Momma with her. By winter, I took a chance that this tenderizing might help me meet my one remaining grandparent, my momma's momma.

"Hey, Little Man," I cooed in his tiny seashell of an ear, "did you know you have a great-grandma?"

Momma took the boy from my arms and announced that it was time for her to make a trip to her hometown to make peace with her mother, like it was her idea. She told me that it had been fifteen years since she last saw her mother.

"She's going to want to see this beautiful baby. You and Becky were only three years old the last time I saw Mom. I think I should drive the four hours to Clearmont and bury the hatchet with my mother."

Usually when Momma mentioned her mother, the sentiment sounded more like a desire to bury a hatchet in the old woman's skull.

This was a calm time, a forgiving time mostly, but Momma still had advice and expectations for me. "You know, they have a nice nursing course at the technical college. I always wanted to be a nurse."

"Then you go to technical college. I want to be a veterinarian, and I'm taking that scholarship, and there isn't anything you can do about it."

Momma continued to hound me to give up the scholarship to one of the church kids. She argued that since the benefactor was such a holy man, God might need to punish our family if one of us accepted money while that one of us still had sin in her heart.

"Remember the story of the Egyptian pharaoh in the Old Testament? You might get yourself a plague."

"Plague? Really Momma? Frogs, flies, and dying cattle—those are perfect problems for an aspiring veterinarian. Momma, maybe God's telling you to let His people go and I'm His people. I'm not giving up that scholarship. I'm leaving in January. Charity has a friend in Langston who said I can stay with her while I look for a job and wait to move into the dorm."

The constant call to repentance and to surrender the scholarship became a frequent theme with Momma all through November and December. At the same time, Becky made random spiritual pronouncements and quoted scripture at will. Sometimes, Becky put her hand on Little Man and prayed out loud, thanking God for her perfect son. The religious jibber jabber and themes of sin and punishment spooked me. I had a premonition that punishment was close at hand. I just didn't know what direction the punishment would come from.

CHAPTER FIFTEEN
JUDGMENT

One Saturday night in January, a week before I was due to leave for college, I got inspired. It wasn't enough to just be waiting for Charity to call me and tell me when to sneak over to her apartment. I knew where she kept the spare key. I planned to be hidden, near-naked, in the dark in her apartment when she got home. I slipped into her place, stripped to my underwear, and sprawled out on Charity's bed. It was a good idea right up until Charity came home and she wasn't alone.

First I heard car doors slam, voices, and footfalls on the outside stairwell. What the hell was I thinking being naked upstairs of Pastor Grind's garage? Would he believe that I had changed my mind about an immersion baptism, advanced fire insurance for the formerly sprinkled?

It wasn't Grind.

It was worse.

It was another girl.

I scooted under the bed.

I couldn't make out the exact words they said while they talked in the living room, but once they stood in the doorway of the bedroom, I could hear and see everything from my vantage point under the bed with dust bunnies, stray dirty socks, and a plastic storage box.

The woman was tall—near six foot—and blonde. Her straight white teeth made her look like she was right out of a TV commercial. She cupped Charity's jaw, and Charity put both her hands around the woman's wrist, turned her face, and kissed the woman's palm.

Straight Teeth spoke. "Charity, I was so wrong. I never should've sent you away."

It was Kelly! It had to be Kelly, but what did she mean that she sent Charity away? Charity had told me that she'd broken up with Kelly. The breaker and the broken mattered to me. I wished it didn't, but it did.

Oh God, no. They were dancing. They danced to music I couldn't hear or feel. Kelly dipped Charity and then raised her up again and nuzzled her neck. It got worse. They bantered. They had a history they could banter about. It was a conversation of "remember when's" posed by Kelly, and Charity recalled each incident. I felt sick.

Kelly waved her arm around. "How can you stand being here in this backwoods closet?"

At first I assumed that Kelly had insulted Charity's apartment, but Kelly wasn't talking about the studio. She was talking about Bend and all the people and things here. As much as I wanted out of Bend, I couldn't endure Kelly talking about it like it was nothing. Criticizing Bend was restricted to only the people who lived there and loved it some too. I planned to come back to Bend as soon as I could do it as a certified vet.

"What keeps you here? Leave this place. Come home with me," she said.

Before I had a chance to think about it too much, I scooted out of my hidey-hole. Both Kelly and Charity jumped, and Charity screamed. Then Charity recognized it was just me and not an ax murderer.

"Raine? What—"

Dust bunnies clung to my skin. I brushed them off and tried to make my voice casual. It was hard to be dignified in my underwear in front of a stranger who was movie-star beautiful and had a history with Charity. I settled for brief and to the point.

"Charity is home. She's been home for over a year now." My courage drained away as I compared myself to Kelly. "You two seem to have a lot to discuss. I'll just get my clothes and skedaddle." I looked at Charity. "I'll talk with you later when you're free."

"Ah, you must be Stormy," Kelly said.

Now that obvious, cheap insult pissed me off. I stood up straighter, picked up my clothes, but held them to my side. I had a body that God had made. Charity had said so. I pointed my perky breasts at Kelly. My nipples were like bullets, and I reminded myself that Charity had been with me since she'd come to Bend. We had made out across the county.

"My name is Raine, although I am feeling pretty stormy right now. You must be Kelly. What, you couldn't find any girl scouts to seduce?"

"Ooh, I'm wounded. You're adorable. I wish I could paint you sometime," Kelly said, but her face betrayed that I had hit a nerve.

"Yeah, well, I wish I could throw you on a pottery wheel."

"Hello, I'm here too," Charity said.

Neither Kelly nor I looked away from each other. It was a staring duel. I won. Finally, Kelly blinked first, and we both turned to Charity.

"I'm tired," Charity said. "Definitely too tired for this discussion. I didn't invite you here Kelly. And obviously Raine, you were trying to surprise me. I appreciate the effort. I think you both should leave now. None of us need this drama."

She appreciated my efforts. That sounded like a euphemism for being awarded second runner-up. I pulled on my jeans and blouse, slipped on my boots, and put on my parka. Charity touched my shoulder as I passed her in the doorway. Kelly made no movement toward leaving.

"See you at church tomorrow?" Charity asked.

I nodded, leaned in, and kissed Charity's neck before I left. Kelly didn't follow me out. I stood in the cold air and waited. She'd said she appreciated my effort. I waited and waited. The door never opened again. Charity's lights went out. I walked back to where I had parked Dad's truck and drove home.

The next day was Sunday. The last place I wanted to be was church, but I had told Charity I would be there. So I went to church and fidgeted. I could have sat with Momma, Dad, Kenny, Becky, and Little Man. There was room for me, and I might have taken some comfort or at least distraction from being close to Little Man, but I was preoccupied. I looked for Charity in the sanctuary during the service and downstairs in the Sunday school rooms, but she wasn't there. Jolene played piano that day, so she was sequestered up front by her dad. I couldn't ask her where Charity was or if she was coming late.

Nails bitten, swivel-headed, I sat through a long church service and marathon sermon. Pastor Grind expounded on the sins of Sodom and Gomorrah, which he hammered on more often than any story except Abraham's near killing of his son, Isaac. I wondered if he would ever get beyond those reruns.

When the service finally ended and I was just a few feet from fresh air, Jolene stopped me and gave me a note. "Don't read this until you're home. Promise me."

"Okay. I promise." I stuffed the note in my pocket. "Where is Charity?"

Jolene shook her head and scuttled off without answering. Pastor Grind grabbed me by the sleeve and motioned for me to follow him to his office.

I stared at him. I searched for any physical traits he'd passed on to Charity. I felt more generous toward him knowing he had helped make someone so beautiful, kind, and queer. I appreciated his genetics. I noted how his hair was a dull brown like my own. He didn't have Charity's perfect nose. His nose was squat like mine. I chalked up the missing likeness to Charity's good fortune to take after her mom more than her dad.

Monstrous bookcases bordered every wall of Pastor Grind's small paneled office. There were more books than I thought it possible to read, especially if they were all about God and sin. Some books were thicker than my head. As I scanned the room, I startled. We weren't alone.

J.C. McGerber, Bend's philanthropist extraordinaire, was sitting in a brown vinyl upholstered club chair at Grind's right-hand side. I suppose McGerber was Jesus to Grind's perception of himself as God Almighty. McGerber didn't acknowledge me. The balding elder patriarch had pockets bulging with hard candy, butterscotch and peppermints he gave out to children at church. I probably had a couple of cavities attributable to his Willy Wonka philanthropy.

McGerber seemed fascinated by something on the heel of his shoe. He scrutinized the spot with his leg crossed over the other leg at the knee.

Pastor Grind scraped a tan folding chair across the linoleum, put it in front of his desk, and closed the office door. I sat in the cold, hard chair and waited for the old man to say something like, *Why, aren't you the intelligent young girl who is going to make good use of my scholarship? I understand you want to be a veterinarian.* Nothing.

Pastor Grind wedged himself behind his desk and plopped into an overstuffed, high-back office chair.

"Well, I'll come to the point, Lorraine," Pastor Grind said. "I've known your mother since we were both teenagers, and I've known you and your sister since before you were born. It's a shame that Becky didn't win that scholarship, but rules are rules."

McGerber sighed and shifted in his chair. He found something equally interesting on his other shoe. I hoped it wasn't my future he was scraping away at like used gum or wet tar.

"Which brings me to you, Lorraine. As you know, there is a morality clause in the McGerber scholarship guidelines. Those guidelines don't allow the money to go to a girl pregnant out of wedlock or any person of questionable moral character. I received a disturbing phone call today—this morning actually—informing me that you . . ." Pastor Grind stumbled here, which I knew wasn't like him, because he had memorized all the sins and likely much of the penal code. "You have unnatural desires, Lorraine. I have learned that you have homosexual leanings."

Leanings? Hell, I'd fallen all the way over.

"I had no choice but to inform Mr. McGerber. As a consequence, he has decided to withdraw his offer of a scholarship to you, and I have informed your school that you no longer have that money available to you. You'll get a letter, but essentially, your registration has been canceled as you would expect. I wanted you to know now so you can make other arrangements for your f-f-future." Pastor Grind's words bumped and skipped out of his mouth, but each one landed like rocks against me.

What future? Bussing tables with Momma?

I wanted to ask him what "arrangements" he thought I could make. I had planned to leave in the next week and apply for jobs near the school, but without the scholarship, I wouldn't have enough money to start school and pay for housing. How could he cancel my application and acceptance to college? The college didn't need to know I didn't have the money. That was my business.

My body lost all air and hope like I had fallen from a great height. Still, my ass was glued to that metal folding chair. I couldn't stand. How could I lose so much in less than twelve hours?

McGerber growled, placed both his feet on the floor, and stood. He nodded at Pastor Grind and left the office. He seemed indignant when he left, like it was his future that had been snatched away from him instead of mine. I was glad he didn't offer me a hard candy. I would have told him to shove it up his ass.

Morality claws. I pictured a beast with wings and muscled legs and arms, and torn flesh stuck between jagged teeth and nails. It had swiped the same opportunity from my family twice. Before I could pry myself from the metal chair and run from the church, Pastor Grind tried to counsel me. He moved from behind his desk and sat casually on the corner of it, his holy crotch level with my eyes.

"This news must be terribly disappointing, but not as disappointing as your sin before God. Lorraine, if you want to pray with me or review scriptures together so that you can fully understand God's position on homosexuality, I will delay my dinner and spend time with you. Perhaps your parents could join us."

His attempt at comfort and offer to pray with me was the momentum I needed. I launched out of that chair. I wanted nothing to do with the God that Pastor Grind hid behind to throw his rocks. I wanted nothing to do with him.

"This is bullshit."

Pastor Grind slung one more brimstone on behalf of himself, God, and whoever made that phone call. "Lorraine, I had thought you, Charity, and Jolene would be a blessing to one another. In light of your sin, I'll expect you to stay away from my daughters, n-n-naturally."

I left the office and slammed the door on the way out. I wished I'd grown up the kind of person who felt justified in property destruction when my anger was kindled. I would have torn up the place, but that wasn't who I was brought up to be. And besides, I'd be damned before I gave up the little money I'd already saved to pay for correcting a tantrum. That money was for getting out.

Momma and Dad had already said their good-byes and given and received kisses from Becky, Kenny, and Little Man. They waited for me in the car.

Dad offered to let me drive. Momma didn't object. Looking back, that should have been a clue to me. If Momma had given me a crumb in those days, I should have checked it for rat poison.

"No, I'm too mad to drive." I got in the backseat, slammed another door, and nearly ripped the seat belt off its anchor.

"What's got you in such a state?" Dad asked.

"You won't believe it. It's such bullshit!"

Still no response from Momma.

"Grind just told me somebody called him and told him I have unnatural desires—I'm homosexual. Now, McGerber won't give me the scholarship either. It's not fair. Becky and I had the highest grades. It shouldn't mean anything that she's pregnant or that I'm queer. Not only that, Grind told me that I can't see Charity or Jolene anymore."

"Jesus Christ. I don't believe it. Who would call Grind?" Dad put the car in gear, used the wipers to clear the dusting of snow off the windshield, and started down the road. He stared out the front window of the car and gripped the steering wheel at ten and two. "Oh, Lorraine, I'm sorry you lost—"

Momma butted in. "I called him."

"What?" I couldn't believe what I'd heard.

"Oh, Peggy, no—" Dad started.

"I said I called Pastor Grind. Last night, you came home late. Your blouse not even buttoned to at least hide something you've done. What would people think? Being with his daughter! He needed to know the truth. It's McGerber's money, and he needed to know the truth and make his decision based on the truth."

Momma cried into a tissue like she was greatly harmed, but still managed to pull out her notebook and write a few things down.

"Remember to congratulate Jolene. She's next in line for the money." Momma spoke the words with some type of emotion, but no remorse that I could detect.

"Stop the car, Dad." Again, a big cow had rejected one of her twins.

"Why?"

"Stop the goddamn car or I'll jump right now."

The snow-packed gravel shoulder crackled under the weight of the station wagon and its cargo as Dad pulled the car from the slippery blacktop. I got out.

Dad rolled his window down. "What are you doing?"

"I will not ride home with her. She's gone too far. I can't ride in the same car with someone who hates me."

"It's three and a half miles home, Lorraine. For Christ's sake, it's ten degrees outside."

"I know that, and I've walked it before and I'll walk it now. When I get home, I'll decide what I'm going to do, but I will not ride with her."

Dad waited a couple of beats, looked at Momma. She kept her eyes straight ahead. "Take me home, old man."

They drove away.

I dug out the note Jolene had given me. I thought I might as well take all the poison at once.

Dear Raine,

I am so sorry about last night, about everything. What a coward I am—I should be telling you this in person.

I'm going back to St. Paul with Kelly. I don't know that I will stay there, but I have to figure this out and can't do it from here.

Don't hate me. This isn't about anything you did wrong. There's just some things I left unfinished trying to please everybody else.

Keep your heart open. I will be braver soon.

Charity

CHAPTER SIXTEEN
THE PARABLE

C harity had gone back to Kelly. Would the pain never stop? I felt like an inept boxer. Uppercuts and blows came at my body from all directions. I hadn't blocked one punch. I hadn't even bothered to cover up. The sad score scrolled through my head: Momma had betrayed me, McGerber had taken back the scholarship, Grind said I couldn't see Jolene or Charity anymore, and now Charity had chosen Kelly over me. I knelt in the snow, too sad and dehydrated to cry anymore.

Before I could calculate the time I would need to be released by the blessing of hypothermia, Dad pulled up in his pickup. He'd dropped Momma off at the farm, switched vehicles, and come back for me. My dad would try to keep me alive the way farmers had to bottle-feed the rejected calf.

He pulled the truck to the shoulder and put it in park, then opened the driver's-side door but slid across to the passenger seat. Although I questioned his judgment in wanting me to drive, it felt good to have some power in my hands. I didn't know how fast that beat-up truck could really go, but I had half a mind to find out, and never drive home again.

As I drove I had awful, violent fantasies about Momma. I pictured her hog-tied and gagged with pus oozing from maggot-infested boils that she couldn't reach to itch or clean. I pictured Momma dead.

"I hate her, Dad. I know you love her, but I hate her and don't try to talk me out of it today. And no goddamn animal stories. I already know some of them eat their young."

"I honestly didn't know that she'd done it," he said. "I'm sorry."

"She's not sorry. Why should you be sorry?"

"No, I didn't rat you out to Grind, but I haven't done enough either."

The roads by Bend were windy and ice covered, and the ditches were steep and deep. Dad said that the guy running the road grader was either shit-faced drunk or dodging gunfire when he'd made our roads. The concentration needed to keep the truck on the road helped me not to cry and rage, but not for long.

"I hate her. I don't care if that hate worm eats me north to south. Damn it all. How can you put up with her?"

Dad didn't say anything at first. Ninety-nine percent of me knew he'd never say anything bad about Momma.

"What do golden eagles, geese, and swans have in common?"

"I know about animals, but, Dad, you have a neocortex," I said. "A higher-level brain. How can you stand sticking with her when she's so stubborn and mean?"

"I don't know much about a neocortex—you're the high school graduate, valedictorian. I do know that golden eagles, geese, and swans mate for life." He took out his pocket knife and cleaned his nails. "I guess you could say when it comes to me and your momma, my brain is a bird brain." He snuck a peek at me, probably to see if I laughed. I didn't, but my crying slowed a bit and I eased off the accelerator.

There wasn't a damn thing he could tell me that day that would make it any better. I knew he would try anyway.

I drove west with no destination in mind except away. When we were past our fields, where Dad scanned the landscape for deer, and when we had passed the cemetery where Dad expected to be buried, he pointed to a gravel road that led away from the blacktop. I turned. He called that road the bunny trail. It was a cross-country route, washboard rough and serpentine. There was no shoulder and the birch trees crowded the road, dropping clumps of snow. The road had been plowed in the last week, but there was only a single car track. The undercarriage of the truck skimmed along the snow. Dad lit a cigarette.

"So, what am I going to do, Dad?"

"I don't know, Lorraine. I hope you're going to go to college." He took his handkerchief out of his pocket and wiped some dust from the dashboard. At the same time his ash grew and drooped from the cigarette hanging off his lip.

"You heard Momma. She called Grind and told him I'm queer and messed up the scholarship."

"Maybe that wasn't the money you were supposed to have. There's people have things given to them, and there's others who work for most everything. I guess we're workers. Your momma is definitely a worker."

"I get that, but how come Momma gets to decide stuff for everybody?"

"She doesn't decide everything for everybody. We can't help who we fall in love with."

He let me sit with those words floating around the interior of the car, every bit as real as the blue-gray smoke of his cigarette.

"Please don't tell me an animal story."

"Nope, this is a love story. I know you heard the story before from Momma, but she tells it too short, and there's more to it. I'll tell it again how I saw it. I fell in love with your momma the first day I met her.

"That day, I was working a roofing job with Twitch. I ate my lunch by 9 a.m. When noon came, I was eat-the-asshole-out-of-a-skunk hungry. Twitch drove and had the idea we should eat at the truck stop. He went on and on about how they were supposed to have a good hot beef sandwich and pretty waitresses.

"I had my doubts about the hot beef sandwich," he said. "They are only as good as the gravy that covers them, and I didn't believe there could be better gravy than my ma's. I had no frame of reference for pretty waitresses, but I was willing to take the risk."

As he told it, even back then, Big Will owned the diner and ran it like a battleship. Dad and Twitch had washed their hands and faces with the garden hose outside the diner.

"I stuffed the brim of my hat into my back pocket and smoothed my hair down with my hands. My work shirt was too sweat-soaked to show the wrinkles it'd had when I put it on that morning. I rolled up the sleeves and buttoned it to the last button at my neck so that my dingy white T-shirt didn't show. There weren't any more improvements possible. I just hoped I looked presentable. I had no aspirations of being mistook for handsome."

I pictured Dad and Twitch as young bucks. I imagined Big Will had inspected them thoroughly like he did the men I'd seen enter the diner. Big Will seemed to be on alert for trouble.

"I spied a table in the back. Twitch tugged my arm and pointed to two empty stools at the counter. 'Better view! Wait until you see . . .' Well he made reference to having been friendly with one of the waitresses the night before. Twitch winked at me and strutted up to the counter.

"He was right about the better view of course. Pies! Blueberry pies, cherry pies, apple pies, cinnamon and sugar sprinkled lattice crust across the top of fruit pies, three-inch meringue floating like clouds on lemon, banana cream and coconut cream pies, pumpkin and custard pies next to donuts, glazed and old-fashioned donuts, jelly-filled and jimmie-sprinkled donuts, long johns with maple frosting and toasted coconut, mashed potatoes, fried potatoes, french fries, hash browns, bacon, sausages links and patties, burgers, roasted chicken and chicken-fried steak, steak with fried onions and mushrooms, pork chops and pork roast. I wanted to eat it all."

My stomach growled. Dad told how yellow-uniformed girls rhythmically whooshed through the swinging door, to and from the kitchen, balancing food pyramids on thick white plates one way and grease-smeared naked plates and cups going the other way.

That was how Dad always remembered Momma—a hunger eating him and just before it got his whole brain, he'd seen her.

He blushed. "You won't like to hear this, but I think a part of you understands. Your momma was so big, curvy, and beautiful. I thought I'd die if I didn't meet her."

He told me that he must have been ready to fall in love, and he fell even harder once he heard her.

"Russ Kringie must have swatted her behind. She stopped, turned, and put her tray on the edge of the counter. The silence, you could feel it, Lorraine. Even the grill lowered its hiss. She said, 'Russ, I know you need that hand to eat, wipe your ass, and maybe even there's some work you accomplish with it, but if you ever touch me again, I will chop that hand off with Big Will's cleaver and throw it in Little Swan Lake for the bullheads.' Damn, if that didn't beat all!

"She moved like honey, slow and smooth. She wasn't like the stick-girl waitresses. She was like the trunk of an oak tree, if it could have curves and softness besides solid strength. She grabbed her chestnut mane, held back out of her face with a binder, and tightened the ponytail, and then took up her tray again and disappeared through the door to the kitchen.

"'I'm going to marry that gal!' I told Twitch right then and there. 'She knows about the bullheads in Little Swan.' I made a plan in my head to marry her, slather her in love and attention, fatten and roll around in her arms, have babies just like her, a big house—a big kitchen with kids just like her, and tumble over them and feed them and feed her and never be hungry again. I didn't know her name or one speck about her, but I knew that I could imagine spending my entire life with her. I couldn't wait to tell her.

"Twitch told me, 'Maybe you should wait to propose until you at least meet her.' Then he waved his menu at another girl. 'Emma Jean! Joseph here wants to meet that pretty waitress, Peggy,' Twitch called out, and a skinny blonde-haired waitress looked up from the cash register, slammed the drawer closed so hard the shot glass of toothpicks nearly fell off the ledge into the bowl of pastel mints." Dad turned to me. "Damn, I like those little mints."

I wanted to punch the lovesick fool, but he just kept talking about meeting Momma.

"She said, 'That is Peggy Larson. Leave her alone. She works hard and shows up every shift. Don't give her any reason to change habits.' Then Emma Jean turned tail and went back to work. I asked Twitch to help me meet her. The rest, as they say, is history."

"How did Twitch already know Momma's name?"

"Oh, they'd met another day. It don't really matter. She loved me, married me."

Dad took a big breath and relaxed with his hands behind his head, and his body slunk in the seat. The grin on his face made me want to laugh at him. He was all gooey when he talked about meeting Momma. It was just like Twitch had said. I guessed it was only fair that Dad had fallen in love the way he did. He shouldn't have to explain it to anyone.

The bunny trail petered out and spit Dad and me back onto a paved road that skirted Will's Diner. The parking lot was filled with the after-church crowd. I pulled into the parking lot, looped through the rows of cars, and parked.

"Nobody decides who we love," Dad said. "That's what I'm trying to tell you, and that's the truth, Lorraine. If a man like me with no education can get a woman way out of his league, get two wonderful children, and this beautiful land, then you can do anything you want." He looked away from me. "You love Charity?"

"Yeah." Nobody had ever asked me how I felt. "But I don't think she loves me anymore. She went back to this other woman she was in love with back at college. Jolene gave me this note from Charity." I handed the note to Dad. "She's gone, Dad. Charity is gone and the scholarship is gone."

"I'm real sorry, Lorraine. I hope you won't give up on any of it. You don't know how it'll all turn out, and sometimes despite lots of disappointment, things do work out like our heart wants." He looked out the truck window a couple of beats before he slapped the dashboard. "I can't explain all the things your momma does. I can tell you she hurts inside and tries to make up for things that aren't even her fault. It all goes back to her little brother dying.

"Sometimes, she makes up by giving away blessings that belong to others. I can't guarantee that it'll help you forgive your momma or even hate her less, but I think it might be time for you to visit your grandma in Clearmont. Take a break from everything. I'll do your chores and make your excuses."

Why Dad thought going to visit my grandmother was important right then was lost on me. I had no nostalgia about being bounced on my grandparents' knees or my hair ruffled by their wrinkled hands. Momma's dad died before she was twenty and by her own report she hadn't seen her mother in fifteen years. But something about the way Dad glanced at me told me that he knew a secret. It was a secret he couldn't outright tell me, but he wouldn't get in the way of me finding out myself.

When Dad and I got home again, I went straight to my room. I didn't speak to Momma, and refused to come out of my room while Momma was home. Momma didn't entreat me with words to do anything differently, but she made fried chicken with mashed potatoes and gravy, my favorite. And she baked both peanut butter and chocolate chip cookies. The sneak.

I was not swayed. I peed in a plastic waste basket and dumped the urine in the toilet once Momma left for work the next morning.

Before Dad disappeared to the barn, he gave me a brown paper sack with peanut butter and jelly sandwiches he'd made for me, and a chocolate bar. "Here's a few dollars for gas."

I wished I could call Jolene. Even more, I wished I could call Charity. Instead, before I left for Clearmont, I called Becky. I caught her in the middle of giving Little Man his breakfast.

"Becky, McGerber took back the scholarship."

"I swear, Lorraine," Becky said. "He looks just like those pictures of Jesus."

"McGerber?"

"My baby's so beautiful."

"Yeah, Little Man is beautiful. I need for you to listen to me right now. I'm so sad and angry." I started to cry. "Charity went back to Kelly, and Momma told Grind I was queer and McGerber—"

"Lorraine, I have to pray with my son. I have to discern God's will for my life. You take care." She hung up on me. I had nobody to confide in. I left for Clearmont.

CHAPTER SEVENTEEN
THE PILGRIMAGE

Clearmont, Minnesota, looked much like Bend. There were businesses—the usual suspects: grocery stores, gas stations, hardware stores, a feed store, a café, and a bar. The grain elevator and the churches were the only buildings with any height, and the school was the biggest and newest building in the town. The nursing home was on the edge of town, just beyond the school, and sited next to a small mortuary.

Would I even recognize Grandma? I hadn't seen her since I was little, and that was not a memory I'd held without the help of Momma and Dad telling it to me. I mostly remembered Momma's tired refrain: *"My folks couldn't abide the decisions I made or the ones they thought I'd made. I'm dead to them and they are dead to me."*

I knew Grandma's name. That would at least get me to the right room, and it wasn't like I was expected to identify the woman in a lineup. Momma's momma was Agnes Larson, and she was demented and half-deaf. The people who cared for her at Clearmont Home for the Aged called her Aggie.

My ruminations and practiced speeches were wasted. When I walked in the room, a silver-haired woman, the spitting image of Momma, looked up at me and smiled. "Why Margaret, I knew you'd come."

I didn't correct her.

"Hello, Momma. Sorry it took me so long to visit you again." I hugged Grandma's shoulders and felt her soft, dry skin against my own. Grandma smelled like lavender and liniment. When Grandma released me, I stared at her, first her face. It was Momma's face with wrinkles, and her hands were big like Momma's, but softer. Maybe hers stayed soft from less gardening. Her nails were clean and polished a pale pink.

"Well, tell me, how's school?" she asked. "When will you get your nurse's cap?"

"School? It's good, Momma." It felt wrong lying to her, but what was I supposed to say? *Grandma, don't you remember that you and your daughter don't speak to each other?* That seemed cruel. Plus, I had only a brief time to find out why Momma acted like a bug had crawled so far up her ass that nobody could find relief. Dad had given me a signal that I was supposed visit Grandma so I could understand something. I listened.

"You have always been a good student, Margaret. You'll be a cinch for a four-year college."

Grandma picked up a ball of yarn from a quilted bag next to her chair. Knitting needles impaled the yarn, and a blue-paneled afghan trailed on the floor beside the bag. Her needles clicked and scraped with practiced speed. She looked at me over her glasses. She said something about Daddy's eggs and William. I didn't catch it. She gazed off and then back again. "That's not right. William's gone now. How silly of me to forget that. How does a mother forget that?"

She hummed a mournful melody I couldn't place.

"Momma, do you blame me that William died? I'm sorry—"

"Who are you?" she said. "You look familiar."

Finally we were getting somewhere close to reality. I took a breath. "I'm Lorraine, Margaret's girl."

"Lorraine, yes, I'd know you anywhere. You look like your mother, but those cow eyes so greenish brown, those you got from your father." She touched my cheek. So gentle. Grandma was back in the present. "That preacher's boy was crazy for your mother," she said. "I think in his heart he wished he'd done right by Margaret, but it was a long time ago. He was older and already had a girl in mind to marry."

Her needles clicked like typewriter keys. Then her ball of yarn rolled off her lap, derailing her memory and the conversation again. She again reminisced about Momma and William.

"Oh they were very close—not like you and your sister, not twins, but only five years apart. Both were our miracle babies. I was nearly forty when Margaret was born and near forty-six when William came along. We thought we just couldn't have babies, and then we had two. Michael was awfully fond of both children, but you know men, they want a son. Need help running a farm and all. He couldn't have been happier when William was born, and he couldn't bear to live when William died. William's death literally broke Michael's heart. Then he died too." Her eyes teared up.

"How did William die?" I asked.

She took a tissue from her sleeve and put it to her mouth. "It hurts me to talk about this."

"Was Momma to blame?"

"Oh no, child! It was an accident. It could have happened no matter who was watching him. Farming accidents happened all the time."

"What happened?"

She stuffed the tissue back up her sleeve and returned to her knitting. Like the needles, her mind slipped and darted back and forth in time.

"It was July," she began. "William had turned twelve the week prior, and he was feeling his oats, asking for more responsibility on the farm and some money to go with that. He was always moving. I suppose all boys are like that." She nodded to me and smiled at the memory. "He was up at dawn most days, working on something one minute, playing with the animals and his few toys the next minute. I remember the exact look of the day, bright, hot, a cloudless sky. Michael and I went to town to sell the eggs and butter, and buy the few groceries we could afford and didn't already grow ourselves."

"How old was my momma then?"

"She was seventeen then. Michael told her to keep an eye on William while we were gone. Well, that was no small task even if she didn't have her other chores to do. She did most all of the cooking then, and that day she was also hanging the wash."

"Momma did farm chores?" I wished I could have seen it all: Momma young. Momma doing farm chores. Momma taking orders from anybody.

"Why sure. You couldn't run a farm in those days without everybody pitching in on everything." She looked at me like I should know more about it, but went on with her story. "Margaret told me how she'd called to William and he'd answer back. Margaret fed the animals, probably weeded and picked the beans and other vegetables as well. There was a lot to do on that farm, and Margaret knew how to do it all. She was always a competent child. Anyway, she called to William and he answered back." She paused and rocked herself before she continued. She eyed the ceiling like the script might be written there or a home movie playing near the corner of the wall.

"But after she refilled the wood box by the cook stove, she called to him and he didn't answer right away. Instead the little devil jumped out at her from behind the wood pile. He asked her to play hide-and-seek with him. She told him she didn't have time for that foolishness and why didn't he help do some chores. But William ran off."

I easily pictured Momma's impatience at the boy's games.

"Margaret got some things from the cellar to make dinner— probably some potatoes if there were any left from the year prior, or some rice and a jar of canned meat. She called to William and again he didn't answer. She thought he was waiting to jump out at her again, so she went on with her work. Later, she called again, and he still didn't answer. I don't think she would have thought to be worried. She sure didn't expect what she found. Sometime during that time, the preacher boy came over—"

"So Momma was being courted by a son of a preacher?" I smiled at the irony that maybe Momma's first love had a preacher for a daddy just like Charity.

"Yes. He was always visiting Margaret. Michael said he sniffed around like a polecat. It was Allister who noticed the upper door on the grain bin was open."

"What—" I saw Grandma's lips moving, but my brain froze at the mention of the name Allister. "Grandma, who did you say—"

"Michael blamed Margaret, and she knew it. Michael told her it wouldn't have happened if she hadn't been whoring with Allister."

There it was again. How many Allisters could there be in the world? What if it was Allister Grind, Charity's dad?

"I didn't believe that was true," she said. "But there was no changing Michael's mind. And then she ran away, got a job at that diner, and word got back that she was pregnant. Michael was even more convinced that Margaret was to blame."

"Allister who?"

"What was his last name? Something." She was slipping again. "I don't recall."

"Do you mean Allister Grind was sweet on Momma? Is he my—"

It was too late. Grandma's mind drifted away again. She mumbled something about a nest egg she'd hidden in the corner of the barn, and her plan to draw a map to it so Margaret would finally go to school. Then, she recited poems or song lyrics that weren't familiar to me. She looked tired—probably from all the time travel. I kissed Grandma's cheek, left the nursing home, and began my drive back to Bend. I had aged a decade in those few hours.

There wasn't a drive long enough to digest that maybe Allister Grind was my father. Did Dad know? I cried for him. Then it hit me that Charity was possibly my half sister. I cried for myself. Charity had gone back to Kelly, and even if she hadn't, how could we be together if we were half sisters?

Back home again, I avoided Momma and Dad by staying in my room. I kept the dogs with me. I cried and brushed the dogs. I cried and kissed them until they scratched at the door to get out.

Even if I had been speaking to Momma—which I wasn't—and if I had the courage and death wish to ask Momma if she had fornicated with Allister Grind—which I didn't—I didn't get the chance because the next day, Becky changed everything.

CHAPTER EIGHTEEN
THE LOST SHEEP

The following morning after my trip to see Grandma, I was in the kitchen when Becky dropped off Little Man.

"Can you watch him until Kenny's done with the barns? Maybe 5 p.m. There's something I need to do," Becky said.

I didn't even get the chance to tell Becky I'd seen Grandma before Momma swept into the kitchen and took Little Man into her arms. Becky bolted out of the house like she'd dropped off small pox.

Momma kissed Little Man's flushed cheeks and swabbed his gums with her index finger. He was six months old and his teeth were giving him a little pain, a little fever, and lots of drool. Momma took one of the wet washcloths she kept in the freezer to soothe Little Man's gums and gave it to him to mouth. Then she put the boy on the kitchen floor and smiled. Little Man sat up, big as you please, and jabbered.

I hadn't yet called Twitch to ask for the job I was pretty certain he'd give me. Meanwhile, Momma was dressed for a long night at the diner. Dad and I had Little Man to ourselves for the whole day. Momma left for her shift without a word from me and just a wave from Dad.

By suppertime, Dad and I were surprised, but not concerned exactly. Becky was an hour late. She'd said she'd pick Little Man up at 5 p.m. Kenny hadn't come to pick him up. When I called Becky and Kenny's house, Kenny answered, but said Becky wasn't home. He hadn't seen her since morning, and she hadn't told him to pick up

Little Man. I told him Little Man was fine, and to send Becky over when she got home.

"Call your momma and see if she's seen Becky," Dad said. "Maybe Little Man is staying overnight and we just don't know it yet."

"Can't you call Momma? I'm not talking to her."

Rice cereal, mashed-up pears and banana covered Little Man, Dad, and part of the kitchen wall.

"I'm a little tied up right now, daughter. Please call your momma and see if she has seen your sister."

Momma hadn't seen Becky.

"Have you called Kenny?" Momma grilled me like I was a six-year-old.

"Yep, he hasn't seen her since this morning."

"Have you called her girlfriends?"

"Girlfriends? It seems like a long shot, but I'll call some people. Maybe Jolene can help me."

"I'll finish the dinner hour, and I'll be home. Becky is probably just at a friend's house and lost track of the time. Don't worry."

Momma must not have taken her own advice, because she arrived home not a half hour after I had called.

"Lord Almighty, how that dinner hour dragged on," Momma said. "Every time the door opened I expected Becky to walk in. The phone rang, and I was distracted to the point that I spilled coffee on my white apron and dropped two plates. Finally, Big Will told me to go early before I hurt myself or broke any more dishes. Now I see I left the diner without my coat and overshoes."

I was on the phone calling classmates in our class and the class behind us. I had split the task with Jolene, who called from her house. Neither of us had any luck, although Jolene said she was asked out four times. There were classmates we didn't reach, and I jotted the names down with a plan to call again or drive by their yards and look for Becky's rusted Chevy Nova.

Reluctantly, Momma called the church, grocery stores, filling stations, hardware stores, lumberyard, beauty shop, and drug store in Bend and called the same businesses in St. Wendell. The feed store and liquor store seemed like a stretch, but she called them too. It seemed unlikely that Becky would venture very far away shopping since it was winter, and I doubted Becky had much money.

It chafed me to let so many people know our business. It probably bothered Momma just as much. After the phone calls, Momma quelled her anxiety by cooking, with the likely intention to fuel our hopefulness with comfort food. She peeled potatoes and set them to boil. She mixed up a cake and put it in the oven. She soaked navy beans. She took ham hocks from the freezer and put them in a stock pot on the stove with some water. She chopped celery, onions, and tomatoes and added them to the ham hocks.

Dad took the last layer of food off Little Man. He hoisted him out of the high chair, bundled him in a snow suit and blankets, and took him to the barn to look at the animals and stoke the wood furnace.

I paced and looked out the window, but truthfully, I was more preoccupied with my own suffering than Becky being missing. It was late January in Minnesota. I should have left for college. I should have left for a city where they actually plowed the streets—a place where winter meant that winter sports were optional and entertaining. I should have at least been keeping warm cuddling with Charity and doing whatever it was queer girls did together, but I was certain Charity was doing those things with Kelly. I shouldn't want to do that anyway because of hell and the possibility that Charity was my half sister, which probably meant damnation in a bad neighborhood in hell. But I wasn't at college, learning, skating, or cavorting. I was in Bend.

"Lorraine." Momma interrupted my ruminations. "I need you to be real careful, but I want you to take the station wagon and drive some of the country roads. Maybe Becky has run in a ditch somewhere."

Glad for the opportunity to leave the house, do something, and at last drive the family car alone, I accepted the offer. I skidded between ditches on slippery country roads that the school bus didn't attempt without chains on the tires. Becky wasn't at the stores I checked, and her car wasn't at the church or the school or in any of the yards of the classmates Jolene and I hadn't reached by phone.

I met up with Twitch in his Jeep at a four-way stop on the edge of town. We talked briefly as snow and ice pelted us. He was out doing the same searching since he'd heard Becky was missing. Becky wasn't at the diner, and she wasn't at Gerry's place or back at Hollisters' farm.

When I got home, the county sheriff's cruiser was in the yard and so was Kenny's truck. I bounded up the porch into the house, afraid of bad news.

The sheriff put his hands on his gun belt. "I told you already, but I'll tell it to you again: I can't take an official missing person's report until said person has been missing twenty-four hours."

He wrote down a description of Becky and her car and took a picture Momma gave him. He didn't seem to take her being missing too seriously. "She's probably shopping!"

Dad got in between the sheriff and Kenny. Sheriff Scrogrum was wiry and strong, but dumb as a post. He had a holstered handgun hanging from his belt.

I wanted that stupid sheriff to know we were the kind of family who looked for our own. "We already called the stores in Bend and St. Wendell. Nobody has seen her today, and I drove around both towns and most of the country roads."

Maybe it was because he was the only one there with a gun within reach, but the sheriff wasn't so set on de-escalation.

"Maybe your wife got tired of smelling pig shit and went somewhere for a beauty treatment," Sheriff Scrogrum said while he eyed the cake Momma was slicing into pieces.

"My wife doesn't need help being beautiful. She's the most beautiful girl there is, and she's not ashamed of how we make our living." Kenny tried to move around Dad.

"Thank you for taking the information, Sheriff." Dad blocked Kenny's path to Sheriff Scrogrum. "I don't want to delay you getting that license plate number and car description out to the state patrol."

Momma put a paper plate of cake in Kenny's hands first and then handed one to the sheriff. Once the sheriff left, Kenny calmed down enough to eat his cake, and another two pieces after that.

After Momma tucked away Little Man to sleep in my room, Momma, Dad, Kenny, and I sat together at the kitchen table. I'd been grilled by Dad, Momma, and Kenny about all the people I'd called and every place I'd checked with the car. With all his questions, Kenny didn't offer a damn thing that he was going to do to find Becky. Finally, he just left in a huff like it was our fault she was missing. Momma and Dad gave Kenny strict orders to call as soon as he heard from Becky.

As we waited, Dad rose periodically to check the phone for a dial tone, as if phone malfunction was the reason we weren't getting a call from Kenny or Becky or anybody who knew where Becky was. All that long night, no one called, and no Becky. One by one we went to bed, but I doubt any of us slept.

At first light, Dad said he was driving over to Hollisters' farm. He wouldn't let Momma or me come along. He was home again a very short time later. Still no Becky.

It seemed like that first day was the longest and also the shortest, because I was the least scared and had the least amount of time to worry. By the morning of day two, I'd exhausted any reasonable explanation for Becky's disappearance. There was some solace when enough time had passed that Sheriff Scrogrum took the official missing person's report. It felt like action, but our family's edges were frayed, and we were not a tight-knit garment in the first place.

Momma and Dad talked with the sheriff about a search party walking the woods and pastures, starting with the Hollisters' place. The fact that Becky's car was missing made that measure an unusual next step. If her car turned up, then there would be reason to do a manual search like that, and the location of the car would guide us to the search area. I pictured Becky's face on the side of a milk carton, and milk drinkers everywhere pitying our family and having profane imaginings about what might have happened to such a pretty young girl.

Momma vacillated between cooking, loud praying, and speculation on what the TV detectives would do in this situation. She said it wasn't fair. They had better clues to help them resolve their mysteries in no more than two hours prime time than we had in the twenty-four hours Becky had been missing.

That afternoon I took matters into my own hands. Let Kenny and Dad depend on law enforcement. Let Momma beseech God, the Law and Order cops, or Sherlock Holmes for all I cared. I knew where to go to hear Bend's secrets. I scheduled a haircut.

"I'm ready for you, Lorraine!" Lucille herded the last bits of hair from Buddy Newman's perfect crew cut, swept them away from the chair, and spun the chair around for me to sit in. Lucille would graduate in the spring when Kenny should have graduated. That wasn't what made her worth questioning though. She'd been cutting hair in Bend since she was old enough to work scissors and clippers and big enough to work the hydraulic chair. Her ears were the only organs larger than her breasts, and just slightly smaller than her mouth. She styled Becky's hair every so often and heard, solicited, and spread the Bend gossip as a part of her vocation. And she was Kenny Hollister's cousin.

Lucille pumped the pedal and the hydraulics in the chair raised me up to the height where she could reach my hair, and I could question her.

"What can I do for you, Lorraine?" she said. "You aren't going to ask me to straighten these curls? That can't be done."

"You are such a tease, Lucille. No, I just want a haircut." I tried to smooth the wrinkles out of the black vinyl smock she had put around me. "Hey, you heard anything about my sister?"

"Yeah, I heard the smartest girl in your class married the dumbest ass in my class, but maybe she's back to being a genius and left the son of a bitch." Lucille toed the pedal and brought me down a notch or two.

"Oh, such language. You make me blush." I wasn't lying when I said she made me blush. I thought that Lucille would have made a great queer if she weren't so certain she should only be attracted to boys. Maybe someday she'd meet her own Charity case and realize she couldn't control who she loved.

"It's the fact you blush that encourages me. I'm sorry. I sure hope Becky is okay. I heard she didn't come home. Can't say that I blame her."

"Becky is over the moon about her baby, Lucille. She loves that dope Kenny too."

"Lorraine, you got to remember, Kenny and I are cousins by marriage." She started trimming my split ends. "I saw him through his whole life. I saw him that day at the beach when he doused that snapping turtle with lighter fluid and then set it on fire. He's a charmer."

I swallowed the vomit that rushed into my mouth at the thought of torching a turtle, but tried to keep the information coming. "Well, you're preaching to the choir. You don't have to convince me she made a mistake marrying him. Becky seemed to think he'd changed and those things happened a long time ago when Kenny was having lots of stress to deal with."

"Stress? Shit! Everybody in this shabby little town knows that Kenny Hollister got beat by his old man every day of his life right after the bastard beat Mrs. Hollister. He'd still be beating both of them now if he hadn't had that stroke and needs them to do everything for him including wiping his hairy ass." Lucille rested both hands on the counter, pushing aside the extra combs, mousse, and spray bottles. She looked at me in the mirror like she was waiting for my response.

I was flustered. I lived in this shabby town and didn't know anything like that about the Hollisters. "Are you trying to say you think Kenny hit Becky?"

"Well—"

"You know for a fact that Kenny hit Becky?"

"I don't know for a fact whether Kenny carried on the family tradition with Becky, but I do know for a fact that his dad beat his mom and the kids pretty regular," she said. "I'm embarrassed to say it out loud because I never was part of lifting one finger to stop him."

I remembered the bruises I'd seen on Becky's arms after Little Man was born. I had never gotten around to asking Becky about them, but I was certain I'd had a twin set the one and only time I had talked back to Kenny.

"For what it's worth, I haven't seen Becky since just after Christmas week when she got the same wash, cut, and set that she gets every few weeks so that she looks exactly like her graduation picture." Lucille shook her head. "Kenny likes her to look just the same."

Lucille painted a picture of the last time she saw Becky.

"Becky acted like she was Miss Scarlett, but pretending that pig farm is Tara don't make it smell any less like pig shit, and I told her there wasn't anything she could say that would convince me that Kenny Hollister is anything more than a bully who's been bullied so long himself he don't know no different. That doesn't go away in a person. You know she had the nerve to tell me she'd be praying for me? What the hell I need her prayers for is beyond me."

Lucille headed back to the sinks. "Come on back, Lorraine. Let's go soak your head."

CHAPTER NINETEEN
THE PRODIGAL DAUGHTER

I told Dad what Lucille had told me. Momma heard too, but I still wasn't officially speaking to her. I also told them about the bruises on Becky's arms around the time Little Man was born. I waited for them to yell at me for not saying anything sooner about the bruises. Neither one did. They didn't say whether or not they knew about Mr. Hollister beating his family, and I didn't ask.

The strain of Becky being missing showed in all of us. Momma was quiet, and Dad was jumpy. I couldn't keep a single animal fact in my head. I couldn't have told somebody the difference between an abscess and an aardvark.

From then on, everything Kenny said or did sounded suspicious to me. Could he really have beat on Becky? Did he know where she was? Gossip mounted. Momma said she heard that Kenny was more irritable than usual. Little Man was still living with us since the day Becky dropped him off and disappeared. Kenny made no mention about picking him up again. Kenny had lost focus on pig farming too. His hired hand called our house looking for him. Another time Kenny left in the middle of chores on some errand, returned hours later, and didn't have the thing he went to fetch in the first place.

Kenny missed filling their troughs and let them get too thirsty. The pigs fought to the point of bloodshed and had to be slaughtered before they reached target weights. The pigs were skinny by Hollister standards. Still, Kenny killed them and had them dressed out at the locker plant. He brought a liquor box of neatly wrapped packages to our house, and dropped the box inside the porch.

"Pork chops are here early this year," Kenny said, and was again out the door.

Dad caught him at his truck before he left the yard. I eavesdropped from the porch.

"What about your son?" Dad said. "Are you going to come in the house and see him or take him home awhile? His grandparents are probably mighty lonesome for the little guy."

"Ma is in no shape for a little one under foot, and I know you and Mrs. Tyler are doing a better job than I could without Becky. Could you just keep him for now? Without Becky, I'm no good with him."

Dad nodded. Even though keeping Little Man was no problem, I think we all worried about Kenny not showing much interest in the boy. I studied Kenny for signs that he'd hurt Becky and kept her from coming home. I couldn't really find the signs, although I didn't know what to look for.

Little Man replaced Becky and soothed my worry in one way. In another way, he reminded me endlessly that Becky was missing. Becky wasn't there to nurse him, so I supplemented the start of him trying solid food with god-awful smelling formula. He smiled, jabbered, and pooped a lot. It smelled worse to me than cleaning up after my chickens, sheep, and goats, but somehow it didn't seem any hardship feeding, cleaning, and loving him. It came natural to me.

I kept my arms filled with Little Man. Even with the snow and cold, I carried him outside and ran with him around the yard, saying we were catching squirrels. I talked to him, kissed him, and said every mushy thing I could think of to him. Soon, I filled a sketchbook with drawings of my favorite little mammal—no raccoons, no mice, no sheep, no dogs or barn cats—only Little Man.

Becky had been gone a week when out of the blue Charity came to see me. Dad, Little Man, and I came out into the yard when her car pulled up. I hadn't seen her since she left with Kelly and I lost the scholarship. She'd been on my mind every waking moment I wasn't thinking about Becky being gone, and even some times when I should have been thinking about Becky. I wanted to run to Charity. I wanted to hug her and kiss her and handcuff her to my arm so that she couldn't leave again, or I wanted to spit in her face for hurting me so bad. I held Little Man as Charity parked and got out of her truck. I pulled Little Man closer and covered my heart. I kept myself from running to her.

"Take a drive with me, Raine?" Her hands were pushed deep into the pockets of her parka.

"I'm pretty busy taking care of Little Man."

"Oh for Chrissake." Dad took Little Man into his arms and shoved me toward Charity. "I think you can spare the time for your friend."

Charity's truck was warm and familiar. I sat quietly as she drove to Bear Head Cemetery, parked on the service road, and killed the engine.

"My father is really mad that I went back to St. Paul. He almost threw me out and told me not to come home again. Mom is talking to him right now, and they are deciding what to do with me."

"You can stay with me. We've sure got the room. Becky is missing."

"Jolene told me when I got back. I'm sorry, you must be worried." Charity reached out for my hand. I had never refused her touch, but I pushed my hands into my jacket pockets.

"I lost the scholarship because Momma told your dad about me. He said I can't be around you or Jolene anymore."

"Jolene told me that too. She's really mad at Dad about all of it. I don't think she's talked to him since except to tell him that he can't pick her friends for her." She nudged my shoulder. "I think you'd be really proud of how Jolene stood up to Dad."

I wanted to ask if there was any reason to be proud of her for the same reason. Had she stood up against her dad? Was she back together with Kelly? I was too afraid to ask those questions.

"I can't believe all this is happening. How long has Becky been gone?"

"A week. There's a missing person's report filed, but we haven't heard anything." Then I told Charity what I'd learned about Kenny's dad being a batterer, and that Kenny had hurt me once, and that I'd seen bruises on Becky too.

"That bastard!" Charity chewed on this information for a while. "You know, maybe Becky just left." She didn't look at me, but leaned back in the seat and peered out at the winter sky.

"No. Becky wouldn't leave Little Man. He was the best part of her marriage. I know it." I tightened up at the suggestion. I crossed my arms, chilled. No way I believed Becky had just left. I also couldn't believe that we were having this conversation and that talking about our relationship was so far down the list of problems.

"Maybe it wasn't enough to make her stay." She started the truck again and blasted the heater.

"Then why didn't she at least take him with her?" I knew my tone sounded snotty.

Charity rolled her eyes and matched my snotty tone. "Yeah, she's just out of high school, no work experience, no college, no money, and a baby too. Who was going to take care of Little Man while she worked some shit job—that is if she could find a shit job and a place to live?"

"Momma, Dad, and I could have helped. We're doing it now." Damn it, I was crying again.

"If she'd stayed here, Kenny could have gotten at her. Maybe she figured at least if she left, Kenny would need help with Little Man and most likely look to your folks for that. And Kenny couldn't beat her if he couldn't find her."

"I just can't believe she'd leave the boy in the first place and then not contact me, Dad, or Momma. It seems cruel." I wanted to say that leaving a note wasn't much better than not saying anything about leaving, but I needed to keep my focus on Becky and Little Man.

"Maybe it isn't about trying to be cruel, but about being desperate and realistic. Husbands kill their wives all the time."

"You think I don't know that? I'm not a kid."

"You said she got all religious after the baby came. If she spent more time in church or reading stuff, she would have heard all that quoting about wives submit to your husband. My dad preached all that stuff every chance he got. Probably gives every man in the church a stiff dick just hearing him say it."

This time Charity caught and kept my hand. Then she ran her finger between my fingers until I couldn't help but clasp her hand in mine to make her stop. "Becky swallowed all that shit. But she wouldn't leave Little Man. That's not the Becky I know."

"Marriage changes people, Raine. Having kids changes people. Maybe Becky wasn't the same self-absorbed sister enamored with the glamorous life of marriage you used to know. For God's sake, she was living on a pig farm. Her husband made love to her and beat her in the same house. She wasn't the Becky you knew for quite a while probably." Charity paused. "Raine, I remember you once told me about mink."

"Oh my God. Not you too. I don't want to hear another goddamned animal story." I pulled my hand away again.

"Tough. I've listened to enough of yours. You can just listen to me for a change. You told me that a mink would chew its own leg off to get out of a trap. Maybe Becky felt trapped and was willing to leave behind something really special to her in order to be free." She looked at her empty hands, but snuck glances at me.

"She could have told us." I hated being mad at Charity, but I didn't like what she was saying. It scared me. I moved closer to my door.

Charity laced her arm through mine. I pulled back, but Charity embraced my arm again and held it tighter. "I can take you, Tyler. I'm an artist. Quit this push back." I relaxed enough to let Charity lace her arm through mine and lower her head to my shoulder. I needed every bit of this touch, but I could hardly stomach the possibility of the truth that came with it.

"If you knew, Kenny'd keep harassing you and your folks to tell him where she was. He'd keep looking for her. Remember, your momma was so set on them being married, she might have even told him where to find Becky." Charity tried again to take my hand. I tentatively let her.

"Momma wouldn't want Becky with Kenny if he was beating her."

"Your momma told on you so you'd lose that scholarship."

The whole thing stung all over again.

"Your folks had to know that Kenny was brought up that way. You told me Lucille said everybody in town knew."

I shook my hand loose from Charity's grasp. "Goddamn it! I didn't know. I didn't know about it. Why didn't I know about it, Charity? I could have—"

Charity took me into her arms. "I know you would have tried to do something if you knew. Maybe Becky didn't want you to get hurt too. Maybe she left to protect everybody. I'm not saying this to hurt you."

It was too late. I hurt too much. I pushed her away. "Why are you even holding me? Where's Kelly?"

Charity let me go.

"I deserved that. I know I have a lot of things to work out, but I care about you and I want to help if I can. This isn't the time to go into what happened with Kelly, but there are things I need to tell you when you are ready to hear me." She drove me home.

CHAPTER TWENTY
EXILE

Becky's disappearance had put our family in suspended animation. Momma, Dad, and I were just going through the motions of living. I released my mice in the barn, sold my rabbits and chickens, and banked that money for college, but the truth of it was that I hadn't much interest in the animals. I needed the energy I had for taking care of Little Man. Dad still took grunt-work construction jobs away from home, but only when Momma or I were home to watch Little Man. Kenny still hadn't said when he planned to take Little Man, he just visited him.

Momma and I only spoke to coordinate taking care of Little Man. At night, after Little Man was in bed, I sat with Dad in the living room where he read books about serial killers.

"Dad, did you know Mr. Hollister hurt his wife and kids before I told you what Lucille said?"

He closed his book and sighed.

"Manfred Hollister. Manfred, now that's a tough name to have—sounds too much like manslaughter. Can you tell I'm stalling?" He went on. "I heard the rumors and ill-conceived jokes about what might be happening on that farm. I never saw a thing myself. I tried pulling one of the kids to the side years ago. They didn't have nothing to say to me. Manfred Hollister was a hard man with a sharp tongue and meaty fists he wasn't afraid to show anyone."

"Do you think Kenny is any different?"

"People aren't set in stone. People have choices. They can rise above their biology and their learning, but some don't. I know you can't probably abide an animal story, but I'm going to tell you one just the same." Dad cleared his throat. "There was a chicken farmer I read about, and he was set on breeding the biggest breasted chickens ever grown. I don't know how they did it—I wasn't there. In a few years that farmer got monster-sized chickens, but it was like both the roosters and hens forgot their mating rituals—they still mated, but the big, aggressive roosters raped the chickens and tore them apart. That was bad enough, but the farmer was so set on getting the bigger birds that he accepted the violence as just part of the process. It didn't even register that something was terribly wrong. The farmer accepted the violence between the birds as long as it didn't disturb meeting his goals of meatier chickens."

"Kind of like people in Bend knowing about Hollister and not saying anything? Grind is so keen about preaching against homosexuals. Why doesn't he rave about violence against women?"

"That's a fair question. I don't have a good answer. You got a good brain, kiddo."

I didn't know or ask what'd happened to those chickens or whether they'd corrected the breeding problem. I felt bad that those hens had no place to hide from those roosters. Was there a place for Becky to hide if Kenny was hurting her? Since Charity had seemed to know so much on our last visit, I called and asked her. She said that the closest battered women's safe house was some place just north of Langston. She came over to my house and we called the hotline listed in the phone book.

Nobody on the hotlines I called would tell me where the place was. It didn't matter that I said I was looking for my sister. There was a rule about giving out the address. How in hell could someone battered get to it if nobody would tell the address?

Charity said that there had to be some way to get there, but you probably needed to be a battered woman to get the map. That gave me an idea. I told Dad that I was staying overnight at Charity's place. He probably knew I was lying, since I was forbidden to go on the Grind property, but he didn't press me for the truth.

Charity drove me to a rest stop a couple of miles out of Langston, kissed my cheek, and then slapped me hard like I asked her to do.

I called the hotline from a pay phone. I told the volunteer who answered the hotline that my name was Naomi Johnson and that my husband had tried to murder me. I needed a place to stay until I could get word to an aunt in Wisconsin who would take me in.

No, my husband wasn't right by me now, but he'd be out looking for me. No, I wasn't currently injured, but I had a good red spot from where he'd slapped my face tonight and some fading bruises if they needed some sort of authentication. They said they didn't—just an identification card. Shit. I lied fast and fairly well. I told them that identification would be a problem because my bastard husband had stolen my purse, and I'd gotten out with nothing but the clothes on my back. Luckily, I lived close enough to the freeway that I could hitch and put some distance between me and that no-good man. I supposed I sounded like a bad movie of the week, but there must've been enough realism, because they let me go on with my story.

They asked me about pressing charges. I told them I was too scared right now. They let it go at that and told me to wait inside the gas station nearby, and a woman named Cheryl picked me up in a gold Dodge caravan.

Charity followed us in her truck.

"What's this place like?" I asked.

"It's safe," Cheryl said. "That's the main thing."

I had naively expected Fort Knox with all the secrecy about location, but the shelter was just a big house called Raven's Nest. Cheryl told me that Raven's Nest was named after a woman who'd done everything people had told her to do when she got battered. She'd told her family, told police, pressed charges, and changed her locks. Her husband had only been in custody overnight. He'd gone from the jail to Raven's house and shot her four times with a gun he carried in his glove box. He'd turned the gun on himself and committed suicide after he'd killed Raven. Their twelve-year-old daughter had been at a sleepover with her church youth group and found the bodies when her friend dropped her off at home the next morning.

Rage coursed through my veins. The bastard had moral dyslexia. If he'd killed himself first, there would have been less pain for that family. Thinking about that family made me think of Becky. Was Kenny that kind of monster? Was he that kind of coward?

The front door of the shelter was locked, and the windows were high off the ground on the first floor and barred on the patio level. A light came on in the entryway when Cheryl pushed a button on the door buzzer. A woman, who I later learned was Melba, peered through the window in the steel door and then opened the door a crack and asked if we were certain we weren't followed.

Let the lying continue. I took a quick glance at Charity's truck parked across the street, but Cheryl and I both shook our heads. Melba let us in. What happened the next couple of hours blurred in my memory and came back to me in pieces as I relayed it to Charity on the ride back to Bend.

There was paperwork and more paperwork. I'd never lied in writing so much in my life. I was relieved when Melba said I could take a break for dinner. Dinner was served in a large family room. Every table was filled with women, kids, babies, toddlers, and older kids too. There had to be near twenty-five women and kids. It looked like a strange sort of convent daycare center—no men. I felt conspicuous, but people hardly looked up when I came in. Another battered woman was no novelty.

I scanned the tables for Becky. Banquet tables flanked the area and were covered with bowls, sectioned plates, and institutional-sized vats of brown soup and steamed vegetables, and a platter of cheese sandwiches. I dished up my slop and took a seat. A thigh-high boy jumped up from a row of benches and shot at me with his index finger and thumb yelling, "Pow! Pow!" A woman, maybe his mom, gathered him back to her. The woman had only one eye. The other was all lid and sunken. Any appetite I had left me.

When dinner was over, Melba showed me a large open dormitory. Then she whisked me off for group. The group leader looked younger than me. The audiovisual equipment was no better than what I'd had in junior high science class. The VCR didn't work. There was supposed to be a film, but it was canceled in favor of something called group check-in, where people said how far they were in their process of preparing to leave. There were more places to be on that road to leaving than I could've ever imagined. I didn't need to memorize any of those details because I wouldn't be there more than an hour.

It was crazy. Every woman who spoke told a story that made it sound like she was married to the same asshole the last woman had described. It was like all those men had attended some sort of trade school to learn their craft. When it was my turn, I said my husband was the same kind of asshole and I suggested we divorce them all— well actually, I suggested we castrate them and then divorce them. I thought I sounded pretty convincing, but after group a woman named Jill came up, told me I was full of shit, and asked if I was faking being a battered woman for a school project. She wouldn't leave me alone. Finally, I told her I wasn't battered. I was looking for my sister.

I dug out a picture of Becky, Little Man, and me cuddled together on the couch at Kenny's trailer house. Jill looked at the picture and said she thought she maybe recognized Becky. She took me to another woman named Rose that she said would remember better. Rose was in the TV room watching some forensic crime show.

Rose said if she ever got murdered, she wanted Bones or the CSI group on the case. She turned down the volume and listened to Jill. Jill asked Rose if she remembered that girl who kept talking about Little Man. Rose remembered. She called Becky a religious nut.

I was finally getting somewhere. I asked when she'd last seen her, but Rose wasn't sure. She said Becky had gone out on a pass and hadn't come back. Rose said Becky must've gone back to Kenny.

When I told Rose that Becky wasn't home and we hadn't heard from her, she said that meant that Becky must be hiding out somewhere, or she was probably dead. I couldn't get out of the place fast enough, but took time to find Melba. I apologized for my deception. Melba was pissed. She refused to check other shelters for Becky, but she said she would leave a message on the bulletin board that family wants to hear from Becky. She said she could leave that message about every woman there.

After Charity dropped me at home, I told Dad and Momma what I'd done. If they were mad, they didn't show it. Dad was ready to confront Kenny, but Momma stopped him.

"If she was at that shelter, that means she's alive. We've got to wait until she comes home or contacts us," Momma said. "I don't want that boy knowing we are on to him."

"What about telling Sheriff Scrogrum?" I asked.

Momma and Dad both rolled their eyes.

"He won't do anything," Momma said. "He's as useless as tits on a boar."

"So what do we do, just wait and hope?"

"And pray," Momma said.

CHAPTER TWENTY-ONE
INIQUITY

Days passed. Becky had been gone two weeks. I hadn't heard much from Charity after the trip to the Raven's Nest. Then she called me at home.

"My parents aren't home. Meet me at my apartment."

Dad dropped me off at Charity's. Her door was open. I went inside and threw the knob on the dead bolt. A sweet instrumental piece played, the lights were dimmed, and I smelled vanilla-scented incense burning. Charity came out of the back room wearing a deep-purple robe. It clung to her body like the skin of an eggplant.

"Hi," I said. "Am I too early? Do you need time to dress?"

"No. I have something for you to wish you luck at college, if you ever go to college."

"What?" I expected a day planner, notebooks, perhaps a backpack.

"Well, I decorated a new camisole and panties for you. I wanted you to have something close to your skin to remember me by when we are away from each other."

Charity was already under my skin. I blushed at the very idea of Charity buying me underwear. I didn't see any wrapped presents except Charity in that silky robe.

"I hope you don't mind that I'm giving your presents a test drive. You'll need to unwrap them, claim them for yourself, but take your time. Jolene and my folks are out of town until tomorrow. You could call your dad and tell him that you are having a sleepover." Charity smiled at me. I suppose she was waiting for my head to catch up. "Oh, you should know that I broke up with Kelly. I told her I want to be with you." She reached her arms out to me.

I had to pee. My heart valves chattered. I lost feeling in my legs, and my lips itched. I walked to Charity, brushed my hands against her robe, and rested my head against her collarbone. Either I could hear both of our hearts or I was having a brain aneurism.

I looked at Charity's face again. I could have looked at Charity forever. She dropped the tie on her robe, and it fell open just a bit. I fingered the slim lapel of her robe as she dipped her shoulder. The robe slid off. I let it fall to the floor. Charity stood before me in a white cotton camisole and bikini briefs. When I finally started breathing again, I laughed and read Charity's underwear.

Charity had copied a poem I'd sent to her. In purple fabric paint, she'd printed our names, places we'd made out and first kissed. Her art detailed every part of Charity's body that I had touched and another dozen parts I wanted to touch. The printing was small, and there wasn't much fabric. It would require some close-up work for me to read it properly.

I traced the words with the tips of my fingers. The straps were slender, like straws looped over Charity's tanned shoulders. I'd seen her bare shoulders before, but at that moment I marveled at the lovely way they followed from her neck.

Charity reached her arms up to release her hair from the binder that held it. The act of raising her arms made me catch my breath. Charity's upper arms had definition, and the skin under them was taut. Even her armpits were beautiful.

Charity turned so I could read the back of her camisole. Her shoulder blades were pressing out against the straps. I put my hands on her waist. She shuddered and said how she loved my hands.

It was like the first time we'd kissed. Electricity ran through my limbs and torso and buzzed back around again like the lights on a carnival ride.

She turned to face me again and then breathed kisses onto my neck.

Shit. I remembered that Charity could be my half sister. Shit. I stepped back. I couldn't believe what I did next. "I can't do this. I'm sorry. You don't know how sorry I am."

"It's okay, Raine, don't be nervous." She touched my face. "I know it's your first time."

"I'm not nervous. I mean, I am nervous, but that's not why we can't—"

Charity cut off my words with a slow, deep kiss that, if it was possible, made me feel even stupider. When I came up for air, I held her wrists so she couldn't touch me anymore and pushed her out of lip range.

"Charity, I can't. We can't. We should wait."

"Are you still mad about Kelly? It's over."

I shook my head.

"Is it Becky being missing? Are you just too worried?"

"No. Yeah. Sort of. It's lots of things." I listed things—things that didn't even make sense to me and probably sounded crazy. "I finally called Twitch, and I'm starting work with him tomorrow, and you know what they say about boxers keeping their legs strong before a fight. The time just isn't right. I'm sorry."

There was no possible way on earth to express how sorry I was that I couldn't read the underwear until I went blind and crawled all over that girl kissing her until my lips fell off.

"Fine." Her tone didn't sound fine. "You at least have to take this camisole home with you." She pulled it off over her head and stood naked except for the bikini briefs.

"Christ Almighty." I thought I'd wet my pants. Here was a chance for sex, and I'd said no. I'd obviously lost my mind. I cursed Momma under my breath. If she hadn't screwed Allister Grind, I could have been making love to Charity.

"I know what will cheer you up. Let me get some clothes on." She talked to me from the bedroom as she dressed. "My timing is all wrong. I don't know what I was thinking. I'm sorry. You're probably still so worried about your sister. Can we just forget about tonight and the underwear? You tell me when you're ready."

Who could forget the underwear?

She sounded all logical and extremely understanding, but anybody could tell she was angry and hurt. Hurting Charity was the last thing I wanted to do. At the same time, I wasn't ready to tell her that we might have the same father. I needed to ask Momma before I put another family into a spin. Pastor Grind might have two queer daughters. Wouldn't that put his underwear in a knot?

"I'm so sorry, Charity."

"Forget about it. Let's go." Dressed, Charity headed out the door, and led me to the garage. Months ago, we'd retrieved four hard plastic garden gnomes and a trio of ceramic mushrooms that Momma had pilfered from Dad's lawn collection and discarded in the garbage bin behind the Quick Mart. Luckily, the lawn litter had fallen on stuffed trash bags. One mushroom was chipped and two gnomes had smears of dried salsa, but otherwise they were just as god-awful as when Dad put them in their yard.

Charity gave a devilish grin and wiggled her eyebrows. "Remember our stash? Let's get them back where they belong. It won't bring Becky home, but it'll make your dad smile. Maybe you'll smile too."

It would be our third time reinstalling lawn art. The beauty of it was that Momma couldn't complain about the reappearing lawn bobbles because then she would have to confess that she had disappeared them. Few things silenced Momma, and the risk of this operation was worth the spectacle.

It was dark. Charity killed the headlights a mile from the driveway and drove by moonlight. We coasted to a stop so the brake lights didn't show. Charity left the engine idling, shifted into park, and switched the dome light off before we opened our doors.

I could negotiate our farm drunk and blind, so I led Charity by the hand. She brought doll clothes. We dressed the gnomes and lined them up along the edge of the snowy driveway with a small suitcase next to the tallest one. We put the mushrooms under a sugar maple out of range of the yard light.

I crashed through the thin ice that covered the puddles in the driveway and splashed cold water into my boots. My dogs must have been in the barn or house, because they didn't bark at the racket we made.

Back in the truck, Charity put the car in gear and accelerated onto the darkened road until we were over the rise and out of sight. She put on the headlights, and we laughed. It felt so good to laugh.

At the edge of Hollisters' place, I saw a truck that looked like Kenny's bucket of bolts. It was pulled over in a gated approach on the wooded edge of their farm. I asked Charity to slow down so I could see what he was doing. The headlights swept across Kenny and his truck.

Satan and Buck tumbled out of the truck bed tethered to a long rope that Kenny was pulling and jerking. He had the rope in one hand and a rifle in the other. In the time it took Charity and I to come even with the approach, Kenny had led the dogs through the gate.

It had been too dark to see where we were putting lawn gnomes. What kind of fool would be out in the dark with a rifle? Charity did a U-turn on the blacktop and we passed by the approach again. I couldn't see Kenny anymore, but heard two quick gunshots, and another shot a heartbeat later.

"Jesus, what's he doing?" I twisted to look back to where the shots had come from. Charity floored it away from the gunfire.

"I don't know much about hunting, Lorraine, but to me it would be awfully quick for him or the dogs to find something to shoot. Do people hunt deer like that?"

"It's not deer hunting season. I suppose Kenny could be hunting out of season. If any dogs could sniff something out quick, it's Satan and Buck."

"Nice names. It still seems like he fired pretty quick if he was hunting anything but his own dogs."

"Oh God, no. Kenny might shoot anything for fun I guess, but Buck and Satan are hunting dogs. Kenny keeps them for their nose and endurance. It doesn't make sense that he wouldn't want them anymore."

"I know this is horrid to say, but what if Kenny did kill Becky? Maybe he's worried the dogs will find her when the ground is soft."

It was like the way geniuses came up with solutions to intricate math problems while they showered or jogged. Charity had stumbled onto something that might explain where Becky was, and I hoped to hell she was wrong.

"We have to find out what Kenny was doing tonight, but I'm sure as hell not going into the woods when he's there with his gun. He'd shoot me and say he thought I was a deer. Hell, he'd likely hang me from a tree to bleed out, and gut me too."

A light glowed through the dusty barn windows when Charity dropped me off at the farm. Charity said she'd stay with me to figure things out, but I told her I needed to talk to Dad alone. He'd know what to do. She kissed me sisterly and left.

I found Dad in the barn. A newly painted birdhouse was drying on the workbench as Dad drank a beer and smoked a cigarette. The end of his cigarette glowed more brightly when he drew on the filterless stub.

"Hi, Dad."

"Hey, I thought you were with Charity?"

"Change of plans. Hard to explain. Hey, how good are Kenny's dogs?"

"How good? What do you mean?"

"I saw Kenny had the dogs out in those woods on the west side of their farm. I think he might have shot them."

"Why would Kenny shoot his dogs? That seems mean and wasteful even for Kenny." He snubbed out the last half inch of his cigarette and dropped it in a coffee can he had filled with water. The butts looked like grubs floating on the surface.

"You think if Becky was somewhere on that farm, and if those dogs had her scent, they could find her?"

"Jesus Christ, Lorraine! What are you saying?" He drained the last bit of beer from his bottle and put the empty in the case with another row of dead soldiers.

"Sorry, it's probably just my imagination getting the best of me."

"Come with me!"

I thought Dad had shut down the conversation and the idea, but instead of retreating to the house he got in the pickup. I hustled to the passenger side. "Where're we going?"

"Let's just see if Buck and Satan are up this time of night."

Dad drove to Kenny's place and pulled up the long drive. The headlights of the truck splashed onto Kenny's folks' house first. His mother's silhouette showed against the kitchen window drapes.

She scuttled to the door, flipped on a yard light, and peered out. She didn't come outside. She doused the light, and I couldn't tell if she was watching from the window or not. The yard light was on by Kenny's trailer, and the changing picture on the TV glowed through the sheer living room curtains. Kenny's truck was parked next to his mom's old Plymouth Duster. No dogs were barking and jumping at the truck like usual, but they could have been in the house.

"Wait here, kiddo." Dad eased out of the truck and left it running with the headlights shining on Kenny's trailer door. He knocked. Kenny answered the door. There was lots of head shaking and gesturing, but I couldn't tell what they said. Kenny backed inside and flipped off the porch light before Dad made it down the steps. Asshole.

"Well, the dogs aren't in the trailer, and I just learned a few things about what is and isn't my goddamned business." He closed the truck door. Before we left the yard, Kenny had the light on again and ran over to the driver's side of the truck and knocked on Dad's window.

"Mr. Tyler, damn it, I was short with you and now you're gonna— I'm sorry. Goddamn it!" He kicked at the ground and ran his fingers through his overgrown hair.

Dad got right to it. "I know you two fought. I got to ask you, son, did you hurt my girl?"

Kenny stared off in the distance and didn't make eye contact with Dad. I could see he was crying.

"No, sir, I didn't hurt Becky." Then he looked down at his feet, turned back to his trailer, and went inside.

As Dad drove away from the Hollister farm, he scanned the barnyard with the headlights as best he could. No dogs.

"Do you believe him?" I asked.

"The place where you saw Kenny earlier, can you see it if you were looking out the window from the trailer?"

"No, it's where the road dips down before Hickman's place."

"Get the flashlight from the glove box."

Dad pulled into the approach where Charity and I had seen Kenny's truck. Dad put on the leather gloves he used for fencing. He started to order me to stay in the truck, but I shouldered open the stubborn passenger-side door and hit the ground running. I shone the light into the trees beyond the gate.

I saw Satan. He was growling, limping, and snaking circles around a black lump at the base of a jack pine. The deep red of the blood was out of place on the snow and drab dead grasses where the snow was already gone.

"Jesus H. Christ! That boy may have shot his dogs, but didn't kill them both. Get the canvas tarp from the back of the truck." He walked slowly toward the dogs. "Here, boy," he called to Satan.

Dad talked quietly to Satan as Satan circled Buck and licked the wound on his own paw. I brought Dad the tarp.

"I'm gonna try to catch Satan and wrap him in the tarp and get him home. After I got him, pick up Buck and put him in the back of the truck and drive us all back to the barn."

Dad wooed and wrestled the snarling, crying dog. When Satan was calmer and close enough, Dad grabbed his collar and wrapped him in the tarp and placed him in the truck bed while I hefted Buck's body in alongside Satan. Satan seemed to calm once Buck's body was in the truck with him. Satan sniffed and licked Buck. He made brief eye contact with me. I could swear I saw tears in the dog's eyes.

I drove home. Once I had maneuvered the truck into the big barn, I closed the barn doors. Dad lifted Buck's stiffening body out of the truck bed and called after Satan to come with him. He lowered Buck into some loose straw, and Satan plopped down next to him. Buck's fur was blue-black from the blood soak. Dad sat down in the hay next to the dogs.

"I'll get him some water. Dad, you got anything left in your lunch pail so that we don't have to go into the house?"

I put the water and meat down by Satan. After it looked like he'd had his fill, Dad talked to him some more while I examined the foot where the dog had been shot. Satan didn't bite me. He just listened and tilted his head.

"You're amazing, Lorraine. I don't think even Twitch could have done that."

"Shot clean through. He'll be okay if we can get it clean and wrapped. Bring me that medicine box and then we better get inside before Momma comes investigating."

"You're right, she doesn't need to know about the dogs."

It was a rare day for Dad to agree to keep secrets from Momma. These were special circumstances.

The house was quiet when we entered. Little Man was in bed. Momma was watching TV. She wore her uniform from the diner, but her shoes were off and she had her feet soaking in a dish pan of Epsom salts and water. She barely looked up.

"I'm not even forty years old and tonight my feet and legs feel like I could be a hundred."

"I'm sorry for your pain, Momma. Good night."

CHAPTER TWENTY-TWO
CONFESSION

All that next week I worked with Twitch. I helped spay and neuter as many pets as the owners would allow and as many strays as I could catch and cage. On the drive back to the farm, I confided in Twitch about Becky having been at the women's shelter. I told him Kenny shot his dogs and that one survived. Dad and I were going to use that dog to track Becky. Twitch offered to beat Kenny for us, but I asked him to wait for further instructions when the search day came.

I was bone-tired when I got home, and it was after dark. I had liked to think that no one could ever catch me the way he did, but the truth was, I didn't see or hear him before he jumped out from the bushes, held me by the front of my shirt, and clamped his hand over my mouth.

Goddamn, Kenny Hollister.

"Don't you dare scream. I'm not going to hurt you."

The damned overgrown arborvitae bushes! I'd have cut them down myself right then and there if he'd have let me go. Sniff and Pants hadn't warned me. They knew him after seeing him so often. Plus, sly Kenny had brought a mess of frozen pork neck bones. The dogs were happy as ticks.

"I got to talk to you. If you promise not to scream, I'll let you go." His eyes were wide and spit flew when he talked.

I nodded a lie. He took his hand from my mouth. I screamed, but he grabbed me again and covered my mouth. I could smell him—his sweat, cologne, pig shit, and bacon. He was stronger than me. He held one hand over my mouth, wrapped his other arm around my torso, and pulled me into the darkness by the house. I kicked at him, but he just held me tighter.

Kenny put his lips to my ear. Goose flesh rippled down my neck and arms. He whispered, "You're my only chance, Lorraine. Please just listen to me, and then you can go into the house. Please."

I turned to face him. He took his hand off my mouth. I could have screamed, but I couldn't break free. Dad's truck wasn't in the yard. My screaming might have brought Momma outside, but what good would that have done? If Kenny planned to kill me, he could have killed Momma too.

"Get the hell out of here. Unless you've come to tell us where Becky is, I have nothing to say to you."

"I don't know where she is," Kenny cried out. He let go of my waist and put his hands to his head.

"You're a liar." I didn't run.

"I admit . . ."

"You admit what?"

"I admit your dad was right. We'd been fighting."

"I already know that, you dumbass."

"She talked all crazy about God. Said God talked to her. She kept saying these things God was telling her to do. It scared me and made me mad, but I never hit her."

"I don't believe you. You're a batterer just like your dad."

"Did she tell you that? Is that what she said? I never beat Becky."

"I don't believe you, Kenny." I wanted to tell him I knew Becky had been at a shelter.

"You know I love her. If you don't believe me, nobody is going to believe me." He dropped to his knees.

Sniff hadn't done shit to help me when Kenny had wrestled me into the dark, but now the whore presented his hairy belly to Kenny.

"I thought maybe you would give me a chance." He stroked the dog's belly and looked up at me. Sniff and Pants had always liked Kenny. Dogs were good judges of character. It confused me that they liked him if he'd hurt Becky.

"You know what it's like to be judged for things you can't do anything about. Becky told me about you." He had tears in his eyes. "I love Becky."

"You have an odd way of loving."

"We got a lot in common, you and me." He stood up. "I just hoped I could get you to believe me and help me find her, but I guess your mind is made up already." He turned and walked toward the road.

I never told Momma or Dad that Kenny had come to talk to me. I waited as an unusually mild February passed into March. The wind dried the puddles, blew the budded trees, and fluffed up the grasses in the pasture. One night after Dad and I had fed and bedded down the secret weapon, Satan, Momma proved once again that she'd never been out of the hunt no matter what ideas Dad and I had. She looked away from the TV and called to me before I went to bed.

"Is that dog ready yet?"

"Huh?"

"I said, is that dog ready yet?" She looked at me over her glasses.

I suppose it shouldn't have surprised me that Momma knew everything, but it did. There was no use arguing the fact. "Yeah. His paw is healed, and Dad's made him practice finding Becky's scent. There were still some of her clothes in the closet, and I found a hair brush she left in her room."

"Get me my duffel off the hook in the kitchen."

"How will we catch Kenny with gardening supplies?" I grabbed the floral canvas bag Momma kept on a hook behind the back door. I tossed the bag to Momma. She pulled out binoculars.

"These have regular and night vision like the military. Good range too." Momma looked at me through the camouflage-colored contraption. "A person could see from the house all the way to the end of the driveway if a person wanted to know if their daughter and her friend had brought lawn ornaments back to the yard, for instance."

She'd known. She'd watched, and she had played along just the same.

"There's one more thing, Momma. I think I ought to tip Kenny off that Dad suspects him. Kenny will give himself away. He's a coward. More than anything he doesn't want to be caught, but we're going to catch him."

"How do mean 'tip him off'?" Momma asked.

"I don't know. I'll just go over there and tell him Dad found his dog and he's bringing him over to search for Becky."

"It's too dangerous, Lorraine. What if he tries to hurt you? Let me do it. Kenny wouldn't dare raise a hand to me."

That seemed awful risky to me, more for fear that Momma would throttle Kenny before she tipped him off and we'd never know what he did to Becky.

Momma pointed at the fridge. "I've got some cookie dough chilling in the refrigerator: snickerdoodles, Kenny's favorites. I'll take him some cookies and then give him an earful about your dad saving that dog for hunting on Kenny's land. Kenny doesn't expect a woman to catch on to nothing, and I can play that part with the best of them. Then we'll watch him from Gerry Narrows's woods. We'll watch him all night if we have to, and we can do it with those night goggles."

Not to be outdone by my momma when it came to gadgets and surveillance equipment, I went to my room and dug through a box of toys Becky and I had had when we were kids. I found two walkie-talkies. Becky's was pink with faded Barbie decals. Mine was army green and endorsed by G.I. Joe. I gave the walkie-talkies to Momma. She put them in her bag with the night-vision goggles.

For once I was grateful for Momma's notebook. She took it out and wrote out her speech.

"So, what are you going to say, Momma? Make it convincing." I made her practice it in front of me.

"Joseph has gone off the deep end this time, Kenny," she quoted. "As if I don't have enough sorrow with Becky leaving town. Now Joseph is talking like a crazy man."

I pictured the dumbass Kenny giving Momma rapt attention between dunking his cookies in whole milk and stuffing his face.

"He's got your old dog, you know, just the devil one—or a dog that looks like him. I don't know, but I think it's your old dog because Joseph is going on about it having the best nose—practically a bloodhound, he says. Anyways, now that dog is ready, and he says he's bringing him right over here hunting. Like we need any more squirrels in our freezer, and I sure don't feel like cooking the rodents. What's that craziness about? As if I don't have enough to worry about with Lorraine catting around, Becky gone, and now Joseph coming hunting here tomorrow with that dog. It's enough to drive a Christian woman to drink."

That was the finale.

"What do you think? Will that speech get him shaking if he did something to Becky?"

"You are a regular thespian, Momma." I touched her arm.

Momma named it Operation Bring Becky Home. I refused to acknowledge that the Becky we'd bring home may have been dead and buried for weeks.

I found Dad in the barn. He was sharpening shovels and spades.

"Momma knows about the dog and what we planned."

He didn't flinch. He knew more than anyone about Momma's ways of knowing things. He walked up to the house. The light in the living room went out, and their bedroom light came on.

A barn cat did figure eights rubbing against my legs while I waited. I gave Momma and Dad time to talk, yell, cry, or whatever they needed to do. Once their light was out, I went into the house and to my room. I had crawled into the upper bunk fully clothed, but still felt chilled. I couldn't stand the thought of bare skin against white, cold sheets. I got up and crept over the baby fence that kept Little Man penned in the lower bunk. I held the sleeping angel close, kissed his head, and whispered, "I'll take care of you."

CHAPTER TWENTY-THREE
THE TRUTH WILL SET YOU FREE

The next day I packed baby bottles of formula and jars of smashed food in a sack for Twitch. He had agreed to wrangle Little Man for a couple of hours while Momma went to Kenny's place, and then we all watched from the woods. Twitch said he'd have rather had a job like beating Kenny until he confessed, but babysitting was the only job offered to him.

"Take him with you to the diner. You'll get plenty of help there from all those waitresses who think you're charming," Momma said to Twitch as she handed him the boy and the necessary equipment. "There are diapers in there, and they aren't just for looks. Make sure you change him."

"What, you don't have this boy doing his business in a toilet yet? What have you been doing with your spare time, Mrs. Tyler?" Twitch took the boy and the bag. He winked at me. "Good luck, I guess."

"We're going to find Becky," I said.

The dust hadn't settled from Twitch leaving the yard before Momma gathered her purse and left to give the performance of her life. I hoped that Momma would stick to the plan. I understood the impulse to beat the truth out of him.

From Gerry Narrows's woods, I watched through Momma's binoculars. She was finished. As Momma stepped out of Kenny's trailer she took off her sunglasses and looked into the sky. That was the prearranged signal. It meant her speech had gone fine and Kenny had seemed to swallow it all. Momma got in the car and backed into his snowblower. Her front bumper grazed the corner of his garage as she left the yard.

As soon as Momma left the Hollister place, Kenny shot out of the trailer and hustled to one of the out buildings just past the garage. He wasn't in the shed very long before he came out with a shovel over his shoulder and pulled on gloves. My breath caught. This was what I had expected him to do, but being right was not satisfying.

In just a few strides Kenny was across the barnyard. He looped around a smaller pig barn. I lost sight of him. Just then Momma came barreling through the woods behind me. She crashed past bushes, sloshed over the remaining snow, and flattened the early spring grasses.

"Where's he at? He make a move yet?"

"He's got a shovel and went around the smaller pig barn. I can't see him anymore."

"Why're we waiting here?"

I was in motion with Momma following in a camouflage slicker she was wearing over her house dress. The hem swayed above her yellow rubber gardening boots. She used her straw hat like a tennis racket—backhand and forehand strokes cleared her path of brush and bugs. We hid behind a clump of elms.

"There he is. Get down!" My clothes sucked up the moisture from the ground as I dropped onto my belly and slithered on my elbows and knees. I held Momma's field glasses to my eyes and whispered a narration of Kenny's movements. "He's digging behind the small barn."

Momma's canvas gardening bag had been slung over her head; the strap crossed her front and back from shoulder to right hip. It was pinned beneath her now, but she rolled to the side, released the buckle, and dumped the contents on the ground between us. Momma had six Nut Goodie bars, a nail clipper, a warm can of diet cola, and the Barbie walkie-talkie. She said she'd given the other one to Dad.

Momma squawked into the pink plastic thing. "Joseph, can you hear me? It's Peggy."

There was some crackling sound, but no word from Dad.

"Drat. Barbie's got shit for range," Momma said.

"Go get into range to tell Dad that Kenny is digging. He'll get the sheriff, or I'll go back there myself so Kenny doesn't take her before we can catch him."

She rumbled off.

As dirt flew from Kenny's shovel, I crept catlike out of Gerry Narrows's woods. Kenny didn't look up. I stopped at the edge of the tree line. Only thirty yards of shin-high grasses, clumps of snow, and mud separated me from Kenny. I positioned myself behind a scruffy jack pine, then watched and waited.

Kenny'd thrown down his shovel and pulled something from the ground. It was blue and red, maybe a tarp or sheet, and it appeared to be wrapped around something or somebody. I dropped to my knees with dry heaves. I wanted to pass out into an unknowing coma or run down the hill and beat Kenny's head in with his own shovel. Instead, I wiped my mouth on my sleeve and stepped a few feet back into the woods.

When I turned back I couldn't see Kenny. An engine sputtered and raced. Kenny had started his piece-of-shit diesel pickup. When it didn't warm up enough to stay started on the first crank, he floored it still in park and filled the air with blue smoke. Kenny drove his truck around the small barn to where he'd been digging.

Kenny hefted the bundle to the tailgate and leaned it against the truck. The bundle was stiff and upright. He climbed into the bed of the truck and dragged it toward the cab. There he let his end thud against the truck bed floor. He scuttled over the side and closed the tailgate. He'd barely driven around the small barn into the main yard when I saw our blue-paneled wagon barreling into the yard from the blacktop. Momma was at the wheel.

I peeled Momma's bag off my shoulder, left the binoculars, and ran full-out.

The two faced off—Kenny in his truck and Momma in the wagon. There were two possible escape routes from that yard, and Momma was blocking one. To her near right and Kenny's far left was an overgrown logging road. Kenny's truck had enough clearance for that rutted track. He accelerated toward it, but Momma was closer and blocked his path, putting her car right on the logging road with no clearance for a bicycle between her and the trees on either side of that old road.

"Way to go, Momma!"

Momma's maneuver was no reason for celebration. By blocking the logging road, she had given up her position in the driveway leading to the main road. Kenny jerked his wheel right and floored his engine. Momma still had distance on her side, but she was pointed the wrong way. There was no time or room to turn around. If she was going to block or slow Kenny from getting down the driveway, she would need to do it in reverse.

She lurched the wagon forward and then shot backward out of the logging road between trees and fence lines and the propane tank. She raced parallel with Kenny down the drive backward. Mud and slush flew in every direction. At the last possible moment, before she would have hit the ditch embankment by the main road, she accelerated again and backed that wagon right into Kenny's front fender. Kenny crashed his truck into the painted boulder at the end of the drive. Momma flattened Kenny's mailbox.

Steam billowed from the truck's crushed radiator, and other fluids poured from his engine and pooled on the remaining snow and gravel. Kenny slumped over the steering wheel, squealing and whining.

Dad and the sheriff drove up. Dad jumped out. The sheriff called for an ambulance on his radio.

The passenger side of the station wagon was knitted against Kenny's truck. I ran to the driver's-side door, worried that backing up had finally killed Momma. Momma couldn't open her door herself, but she was alive.

"Momma, are you all right?"

"Lorraine, Lorraine. I can't move. Maybe my spine is split. Maybe I've been shot. Maybe my innards have ruptured. I have such pain right here." Momma felt low on her belly, and I halfway expected her to hand me her spleen.

Then Momma smiled at me. "Oh. I forgot to unhook my seat belt."

Once unbuckled, Momma rolled down on the seat and put her arms out to me. I wrenched her out like she was a newborn calf. Momma kicked and pushed with her feet against the floor of the car first and then the inside of the door. She stretched her legs and climbed out of the car. I helped her to her feet and got her dress back down from the hip regions where it had migrated.

Dad and the sheriff peered over the side of Kenny's truck bed.

"He's got a tent wrapped around something." Sheriff Scrogrum climbed into the truck bed. He kneeled and looked at Dad. "Now Joseph, you don't need to see this right yet. We don't even know what's in here."

"Sheriff, I do need to see it, and right now." Dad climbed up on the truck bed.

Momma grabbed me by the shirt, tucked me into her bosom, and laced her arms around me. I rested in Momma's arms for the first time in a long time. I knew Momma was broader, but I'd forgotten that she was also taller than me. She sheltered me, and I covered her heart.

Sheriff Scrogrum knifed through what appeared to be electrical cords and tent straps tied at varying intervals. He pulled at the material, but eventually used the knife to cut the plastic tarp. He shrank back from whatever smell wafted from the opening.

"Sorry." Sheriff glanced at Dad.

Dad reached over and tore at the fabric.

Kenny whimpered in the truck. "Ain't someone going to get me a doctor?"

"You should have worn your seat belt!" Momma yelled and squeezed me tighter.

"What in the hell?" Dad said, and he and the Sheriff looked at each other.

I extricated myself from Momma. I had to know. I ran to the side of the truck and hoisted myself up so I could see over the side. Momma followed me and did the same. The smell was sharp and sour. My brain was muddled. I knew I was looking at a person, a dead person for certain, but it wasn't Becky.

"It ain't Becky! It ain't Becky." Dad cried, laughed, and scratched his head.

"Who is that?" I asked.

Sheriff Scrogrum stood up in the back of the truck. He addressed the assembly.

"I can't say for certain. I'm no forensic expert, but my guess is that if I were to go up to the main house, old man Hollister isn't home."

Once Momma and I were back on the ground, Dad came over and put his arms around us. "It ain't Becky. There's still a chance," he said.

"Oh thank God! It's going to be okay, Joseph. I just know it." Momma patted his back. "God is good. God forgives."

Gush and hugs would have to wait. I confronted Kenny. "Where is Becky? Did you kill your dad?"

"I didn't kill nobody." He held one arm against his ribs and wiped his bloody lip with the back of his hand.

"You killed one of your dogs, and nearly killed them both."

"I didn't kill my dad, and I didn't hurt Becky." Tears filled his eyes.

Sheriff Scrogrum marched up to the main house to ask Mrs. Hollister some questions. When he got back, he told Momma, Dad, and me that Mrs. Hollister had a hell of a story to tell. The old man had fallen and cracked open his skull. She swore there was no murder, just a quick burial.

"I don't think anybody killed the man. Mr. Hollister had been sick a long time and dodo-headed since his stroke several years back. He probably died of natural causes." Sheriff Scrogrum speculated further that after old man Hollister died, Kenny got scared and buried him to make sure his social security check kept coming to Mrs. Hollister. "God knows she had at least that coming to her for all the years she lived with that cuss, and then had to take care of him when he had no control of his senses, let alone his shit and piss. Pardon my French."

Sheriff Scrogrum turned to Dad. "At any rate, Kenny will do some jail time for hiding the body, illegal burial, and whatever else the county attorney can come up with to keep him off the place. You file for temporary custody of that little boy. While Kenny's gone, let that dog have a sniff. Mrs. H won't give you any trouble. She's pretty worried about a trip to the pokey for cashing those checks."

It was another half hour before the ambulance got there. The medics put the body in the back of the ambulance before they took a look at Kenny.

"He gonna live long enough for me to get him to jail?" Sheriff Scrogrum hovered by the medics. When the medics said Kenny would be sore, but fine, Sheriff Scrogrum put him in the back of his squad car.

What was I supposed to do now? Celebrate the nearly missed tragedy? Momma, Dad, and I went home, but Dad didn't stay home. He had asked Twitch for the use of his backhoe when Twitch had brought Little Man back to the farm. Twitch wasted no time in getting the machine over to Dad. Twitch offered to help, but Dad flatly refused.

"I have to do this myself."

Dad's words were clear, but I defied him. I hustled back through the woods to watch him. I justified my sudden departure by telling Momma I needed to retrieve her binoculars from where I'd left them.

Dad took Satan back to the same spot behind the small barn where Kenny had dug up the rotting corpse of Mr. Hollister. After Satan scratched in the dirt and ran in circles, Dad tethered the dog to a tree away from the area. He dug all along the small barn and about five feet into the surrounding yard. He dug down eight feet or so where he could. The blade of the backhoe scraped against the remnants of what I guessed was an old barn foundation. There was probably no way that Kenny could have made any more headway with just a shovel, and he didn't have any heavy equipment except a small front loader he used to clean barns and move snow.

Dad stopped digging. His shoulders slumped, and he removed his hat, wiped his forehead, wiped his eyes, and blew his nose with his handkerchief. He loosed the dog and drove the backhoe back to the farm. I made sure I was seated in the kitchen with Momma when he returned.

"Nothing," Dad said when he came in the kitchen and made brief eye contact with Momma. Momma had Little Man on her lap, but passed the boy off to me.

"Take that boy in the living room and let him practice cruising the couch and chairs," Momma said. I left the room with Little Man and without argument, but I positioned myself so I could see and hear Momma and Dad.

Dad washed his hands and arms in the kitchen sink and dried them with the towel that hung decoratively from the handle of the stove. Use of that towel usually got the user an earful from Momma. Silence hung in the air until she broke it.

"Just say it, Joseph. I know you blame me for Becky being gone, maybe dead."

"I don't blame you. I blame Kenny Hollister," he said. "Eventually, he's going to get caught, and I want to be there when it happens. He'll spout some shit about losing control, but Christ knows he only lost control when he was raising his fists to his hundred-and-ten-pound wife. He never punched the bruisers he hung out with or the cops with guns who pulled him over every so often. He had control not to hit them."

Gerry came to the door with a Tuna Helper hot dish. She hadn't visited at all since Becky had gone missing. Momma looked at Gerry through the window. She turned back to me and said that she wanted nothing to do with fair-weather friends or anyone being a spectator to our grief. I knew she wouldn't be inviting Gerry into our house. Momma opened the door, took the package from Gerry, thanked her, closed the door without explanation or apology, and threw the food in the trash. "Road kill helper, no thanks."

Leaning against the kitchen counter near the refrigerator, Dad said, "Peggy, I don't blame you for her disappearance. I won't say she's dead. I don't blame you for her being gone, but by God I blame you and your religion that pushed them to get married." He was red-faced and he set his jaw. He opened the refrigerator and scanned the shelves as he spoke. "Becky thought it was more important to be married—period—than married to someone who'd treat her right, and once she done it, the church kept her there being beaten as surely as the church was a live trap—stay and die or cut off her own foot to maybe get away."

"A baby needs a father, Joseph. Not everybody gets to marry their dreamboat. Some people settle for what seems good enough at the time."

"By God, I never settled. I married the woman I fell in love with the first time I saw her at a little country diner. I still love that woman with my whole heart though she hasn't ever made it easy, God knows." His voice sounded cracked and ragged. He opened drawers and cupboards and then slammed them closed.

"You settled, Peggy, and you got it in your head that everybody's done the same thing. I'm sorry I wasn't your first choice—your dreamboat—but he didn't step up, Peggy. I did, and you married me and raised kids with me, and for God's sake, I hope someday you can make peace with your choices." He moved to the dining room and abused the drawers and doors on the buffet.

"How dare you accuse me of not making peace with my choices! I'm here every day for you and our girls, Joseph." She pounded her fists on the table. "And I am sober."

"Yeah, throw that into my face. How convenient for you that I drink—makes me an easier target than you, the Holy One."

The tone he used surprised me.

He went on. "Speaking of which, where'd you put it?"

"It's in the toilet tank."

"Thank you, at least it should be cold."

Dad went into the bathroom and came back to the kitchen with a six-pack of Grain Belt Beer. He sat at the kitchen table across from Momma, put the beer down, and pulled one can loose from the plastic loops. He took a big swig.

"Ahhh." He peeked at Momma. "You keep looking back, searching for how you can make it all turn out differently. Marrying that old boyfriend wouldn't have kept your little brother from dying in that corn bin, and it sure as hell wouldn't have kept your folks from blaming you for it. Their hearts were set."

His chair scraped across the floor as he moved closer to Momma. I craned my neck to take it all in. Dad touched Momma's hair. He cried. Momma cried too. Dad slid off his chair, dropped to his knees in front of Momma's chair. He bowed his head. "Those old regrets won't bring William back, and they won't bring Becky home." He laid his head in her lap.

Momma raised her hands like it was a holdup. She picked some lint off Dad's collar, petted his head, and ran her hand along his neck. I swore Dad was purring. Momma's face contorted, her lips tightening and then puckering, and she smoothed his hair and kissed the crown of his head. She raised his face between her hands and kissed the tip of his nose and finally his lips.

"Old man, you infuriate me, but I know my life is with you, and I don't need to make over the past, especially where you're concerned. I may act like I do sometimes, but I have everything I need right now, especially if we can find my Becky. Now go get Little Man and give Lorraine a break. You show that boy how to paint some of those wooden cages you call birdhouses."

Dad rose up and laughed. "You just don't appreciate my art."

"Yeah, that's it," Momma said.

Once Dad and Little Man were outside, I took a chance at asking Momma for the truth. "Who was dad talking about?"

Momma lifted the coffeepot and tipped it upside down over her cup. A drip or two fell in. She mechanically measured out fresh coffee grounds, let the tap run until the water was cold, and filled the coffeepot. The lid rattled as she worked it into the opening and carried the pot to the stove. Her hands shook. The water on the outside of the pot hissed when the gas flames licked it up.

I planted myself where Dad usually sat and waited for Momma to speak. She perched in her chair and stared into her cup. I knew that if Momma was going to push me out of her business, she would have done it already. For the first time in a long time, she really looked at me.

"Lorraine, I wish I had an alibi for my life, something that evokes some sympathy and at least masquerades as an explanation."

As if the day hadn't already had its share of weirdness, Momma opened a can of Grain Belt Beer, took a long pull, opened another one, and slid it across the table to me. I accepted it along with all the other unexpected events.

"Things were supposed to be different. I was smart and obeyed my parents. I was supposed to be a nurse. I thought I was supposed to marry him. I wanted college and city life, to raise a family where there was culture and malls. William was supposed to live and grow up. When William died everything crumbled. I couldn't take my parents' money for school, never thought it was mine before William died and certainly didn't think I deserved it after. I couldn't marry the man I thought I'd marry. I was dead to my parents, but they only had grief for William. So, I left home. I got a job in Bend, away from Clearmont. It wasn't where I wanted to go, but it was out. I got married. Before I had time for reflection, I had two kids."

In my head a voice screamed, *Ask her now. Ask her if the man she thought she'd marry was Allister Grind. Ask her if Grind is my dad.*

"You girls, you have been inside me, seen my innards, and left my body through my intimate portal, but you don't know me and I don't know you. I don't even know where Becky is. It's like once you were feeding from me—sharing my food and blood—and then you were born. I delivered you like a magician pulling rabbits out of his hat and what did I find? I found I'd given birth to bunnies. What was I supposed to do?" Momma swiped her big hand in the air in the direction of the barn.

"Your dad was no help. He did things, but in his mind he believed that you would just turn out if we kept you fed. He believed in hope and potential. Children need direction and discipline too, or they get lost and they die. While he was being optimistic, I had the thankless job of guiding you, which was damn hard work." She sighed and laughed.

"I couldn't get over the fact I gave birth to rabbits. I didn't feel like I did anything special myself, but there you were. You were so small. How was I supposed to know how to keep you safe?"

My chest was tight with heartache for her. "Momma, I'm sorry about everything. I'm sorry you lost so much, that William died, and you didn't get to go to college."

"You're a tender-hearted girl aren't you, Lorraine? I always liked that about you. You're just like your father."

That was as close to a compliment that Momma had ever given me. I locked up. I couldn't bring myself to break the spell by asking about the real identity of my father.

CHAPTER TWENTY-FOUR
POSSESSION

A couple of days passed. While Momma and Dad shopped for groceries in town with Little Man, Gerry came over to our farm. She had a stack of books. When I came to the door, Gerry motioned to me to come out on the lawn.

In a loud voice—not her library voice—she said, "I have the books you ordered."

She'd never delivered our books, but maybe she was doing it because she knew how stressed we were and she just lived the next farm over.

Then Gerry leaned in and used her official library voice. "Make some excuse and get over to my place right away. I don't know if I can keep her there much longer. Come alone."

"Keep who?"

"Your sister."

"Becky?"

"Do you have another sister I don't know about?"

"Wait, what are you talking about?"

Gerry headed for her car like she was running from a fire or going to a really good book sale.

"Wait." I raced to the passenger side of Gerry's car and got in. Gerry did a U-turn in the yard and barreled out of the driveway as I clung to the seat and tried to close the car door.

"Is Becky okay?"

"'Okay' is a relative term." She pulled into her yard. "I'm sorry, Lorraine, she's only been here a few days. I believed what she said about Kenny, and I wanted to give her a chance to make a plan, but then today . . ." Gerry's voice trailed off, and she motioned for me to follow her into her house.

I followed Gerry through the mudroom and into the kitchen. There, at Gerry's yellow Formica table, sat Becky. Her back was to me, but I'd have known her anywhere. Her perfect blonde hair fanned out over her shoulder blades. I recognized the stubborn set of her jaw as she turned in profile. She looked at me. Her eyes were blackened, and she had bruises and welts up and down her arms and neck.

"Jesus Christ! He beat you again? How—"

Gerry interrupted my rant and pulled me into the pantry.

"Kenny didn't do that. When she came here a few days ago, she didn't have those marks and I haven't let her out of my sight except yesterday, when I came to your house, and today when I came to find you. She called me four days ago and begged me to come get her. She had traded her car for time at a ratty motel outside of Langston. She was out of money and time at the motel. She made me promise not to tell anyone. She said her life depended on my discretion."

I took frequent peeks at Becky while Gerry talked.

"Lorraine, Becky told me Kenny was just awful to her, that he was evil and that she needed to get her son away. I believed her. I've researched wife abuse."

"Just tell me what happened."

"As much as it grieved me to know your family was so worried, I trusted Becky. Then I saw what she did."

"What?"

"Becky slipped outside with a knife. She cut switches from the brush and whipped herself, all the time chanting something about the devil and God and your momma," Gerry said. "One minute she's herself, and the next minute it's like reasoning with the girl in the exorcism movie. She talked about how Kenny killed the father and the son wasn't safe. I couldn't make heads or tails out of her ravings. Heavens, she used to like women's magazines. What happened to her?"

"We need to get her to a doctor. Let me call Twitch." I moved toward the phone, but Gerry pulled me back into the pantry.

"Lorraine, this is out of Twitch's league. She needs a head doctor."

"I don't know any head doctors." I called Twitch at the vet office. I asked him to come to the Narrows's farm, and if he saw Dad and Momma, to send them that way too.

"Becky is here and she's real sick."

"Does she need an ambulance?"

"I don't know. She's breathing okay and she's not bleeding, but the inside of her head is a mess. Come quick. I'm scared. I don't know what to do."

I went back to the kitchen where Becky sat. She looked so thin. Her perfect complexion bleached in contrast to the bruises on her face and arms. I wanted to touch her, be sure she was real.

"Becky? Where have you been? We've been so worried."

Becky peered at me like she didn't know me. Her eyes were wide but dull. Then she turned her head toward the ceiling and to the side before she spoke to me.

"Lorraine, I'm glad you are here. You have to help me." She glanced side to side, then leaned forward and whispered, "Gerry doesn't believe me. He got to her. Don't let her know you're going to help me."

"Kenny? You're safe now, Becky. Kenny is in jail. Who do you think got to Gerry?"

"Satan. Sometimes, he got to Kenny too. Lorraine, you can never be sure who Satan takes. He took Kenny, but then Satan gave him back. He's just trying to get me, and he'll use all his powers. That's why you've got to help me." She grabbed my hands in hers. There was genuine terror in her eyes.

I squeezed Becky's hands. "I'll help you, Becky. I'm going to get you help."

Becky closed her eyes, rocked, and prayed.

"I beseech thee, Lord. Protect me from the power of Satan." She spoke the words over and over again. She didn't seem to hear the sound of a car arriving in the yard. I let go of Becky's hands and looked out the window.

It was Twitch. He had Momma, Dad, and Little Man in his Jeep with him. I went outside, not certain where to begin except that I knew that Little Man shouldn't see his mom like she was. I took Little Man in my arms. He was real and just the same as I had remembered. I hugged him. He yanked on my hair and ears as I did some raspberries on his tummy. His few teeth scraped on my scalp.

Everyone spoke at once. With a look, Momma silenced everyone else.

"Where is she? What's wrong with her?" Momma asked, but didn't wait for any answers. Gerry stepped forward and blocked her route to the house, a brave and possibly dangerous gesture.

"Before you enter my kitchen, you need to hear something from me. I've been keeping your daughter at my house for four days. For the worry I put you through, I'm sorry. I believed Becky's story that her husband was evil, and I assumed he'd beat her. I still don't know that he didn't before. The only thing I can say with some certainty is that he hasn't touched her since she's been here, and she still tells the same story." Gerry hesitated. "I saw her hurt herself."

"I need to see my daughter," Momma said. "I appreciate what you've done, Gerry. But right now I need to see Becky."

"Becky is having some sort of nervous breakdown," Gerry said to Momma's back.

Momma stomped up the steps to Gerry's house. Dad and Twitch were right on her heels. Little Man, Gerry, and I stayed outside. I held Little Man. His nose ran and his cheeks were chapped. Momma had him coated temple-to-chin in Vaseline.

After a few minutes, Twitch came outside and interrogated Gerry. "She been talking this religious gibberish the whole time?"

Gerry nodded.

"She really did those injuries to herself?"

Gerry nodded again.

"What does it mean, Twitch?" I asked.

"Well, she's the right age for a first mental breakdown. I don't know enough to tell you the precise name for what she's got, but if I had to guess, I'd say she might have some sort of schizophrenia. Christ, I hope I'm wrong." He turned again to Gerry. "Could you get Peggy, Lorraine, and the boy home again if Joseph and I take Becky over to the hospital in Langston?"

"I can," Gerry said.

"I'm going with you," I said.

"No, you're not," Twitch said. "Little Man and your momma need you at home."

"You're out of your mind too if you think Momma is going to let you take Becky without her."

"Your momma is the general most of the time, but I'm not in her army. I'm an independent, a mercenary, and I'm only taking Joseph and Becky with me." Twitch marched up the steps and into the house.

I handed Little Man to Gerry and followed Twitch. He whispered something quick to Dad and stepped over to Momma, who was crying and hugging Becky.

"Oh, my dolly, my baby girl, I was so scared I'd lost you too."

"Momma, it's so good to see you. How are you?" Becky hugged Momma back. "Where's that Little Man of mine? I miss him."

Twitch leaned in and whispered a longer message in Momma's ear. Her face drained of color. She released Becky, and stepped back against the wall and shut her mouth.

Dad and Twitch each took one of Becky's arms, but she resisted them.

"Get behind me, Satan."

Dad started to cry.

"It's okay, Becky; God led us to help you." Twitch glanced at Dad and nodded. "Sing."

Twitch began crooning the hymn, "The Old Rugged Cross." Dad joined in next, and then Becky. Only Becky came close to the right tune or words. She didn't seem to notice their ill attempt. Caught up in the praise of it, she glowed like someone finally understood her heart.

They walked her to the Jeep. She walked right past Gerry and Little Man. She just kept singing. She didn't run to Little Man and take him in her arms. She didn't as much as smile or wave to him. That told me more than Becky's talk of Satan or her self-inflicted wounds. Becky was very sick.

Becky, Dad, and Twitch left in Twitch's Jeep for the hospital in Langston. Twitch drove and Becky sat in the back with Dad. Their singing faded as they drove away from Gerry's yard.

Gerry offered to let Momma, Little Man, and me stay with her longer.

"Our family has inconvenienced you enough for this century, Gerry. But do come over for a game of Scrabble once Becky's well again and I can think."

"Peggy, you and I are from the same town. We have more in common than we have different. You are no inconvenience to me and neither are your daughters. Get in my car and I'll drive you home. I'll bring some Hamburger Helper over tomorrow to help you through the wait."

"Goody."

Once home, I settled Little Man on the floor with the dogs and a teething biscuit for each of them. I dialed Sheriff Scrogrum to tell him Becky had been found, but Momma told me to stop.

"What about Kenny? He didn't hurt Becky like we thought."

"One more night in jail won't make a big difference," she said.

Of course that was only true from our side of the bars.

It was past midnight when Twitch dropped Dad off at home. Twitch didn't come in the house. Little Man was long asleep. Momma cheated at solitaire while I chewed my nails bloody. Dad joined us at the kitchen table. Out of habit, Momma got Dad some coffee. He looked like he'd been pulled through a knothole.

"Well?" I asked. I had my own idea. While he'd been gone I'd found every book in our house that mentioned mental illness generally and schizophrenia specifically. I found a short article in the World Book Encyclopedia and an entry in the dictionary. Neither gave me any comfort.

"We got her into the hospital, and she was sleeping when I left."

"What's wrong with her, Joseph?"

"They didn't have any psychiatrists on duty. A psychiatrist from St. Paul will drive over tomorrow to give a consultation," Dad said. "The young intern who talked to her called it a psychotic break. She may have schizophrenia. They want to talk with both Gerry and Kenny to figure out how long she's been sick and what all's been out of whack."

"It's something like she hears and thinks things that aren't," I said. "She might have problems taking care of herself and problems getting along with people."

Dad pulled some papers out of his pocket, unfolded them, and slid them across the table for Momma and me to read. I read every page as fast as Momma surrendered them to me. As far as I could tell, schizophrenia was a big wheelbarrow of a disease where doctors threw things they couldn't explain.

"The doctor gave us this information. Near as I can tell, Becky is going to need to be on medicine, probably for the rest of her life," he said. "There's no cure, and the treatment isn't any picnic either."

He rose from the table and said good night. He started down the hall and turned back to Momma.

"Peggy, the doctor said if Becky's got this, it would be helpful to know any family history of mental illness or medications used so that they can figure out the best treatment for her."

There would never be a right time to ask the question I had been both burning and petrified to ask since my visit to Grandma Larson. So even though Momma and Dad were shell-shocked already, I dropped another bomb and waited to see who would be among the causalities.

"I suppose you better tell our father." I looked at Momma and then at Dad.

Dad came back to the table.

"What are you talking about, Lorraine?" Momma asked.

"I'm not a kid anymore. Grandma told me about you and Allister. You should tell him about Becky before he hears from somebody in town."

"Allister?" Dad almost always looked beaten down and tired. Now, I added confused to that list.

I turned to Momma. "Doesn't Dad even know?" I was a festering boil that had reached a head. *Pop.* "Tell him for Chrissake! Tell me! Allister Grind is Becky's and my biological father, isn't he, Momma?"

"What? No." Momma shook her head. "This day has been painful enough for two lifetimes, Lorraine. Don't add to it." She looked down at her hands.

"Tell me. Tell me that Dad is not my father. I deserve the truth, especially now. Tell me."

Momma's hands shook. The water in the glass she held quaked and splattered onto the table. She put down the glass of water and picked up her notebook. Her face reddened and her eyes bore into me as if to stop my words, but I plowed ahead.

"Tell me, you self-righteous, cold woman!" I knocked the notebook out of her hands.

"Stop writing down everyone else's sins and confess some of your own."

Dad slapped me. His open, callused hand stung my face, but the pain in my heart was worse. He grabbed me by the shoulders and yelled in my face. "I am your father. I am Becky's father. I have always been—"

"It wasn't Allister Grind," Momma began. "Allister Grind was married and already had Charity before I met your father. I never in my life had sex with Allister Grind."

That was a relief. I felt a little stupid that the math hadn't occurred to me already, and I felt damn ignorant thinking I'd missed the opportunity to make love with Charity because I thought we were half sisters.

Dad let go of me. "Peggy, you don't—"

"No, Joseph, I do."

Dad went to Momma's side and stood behind her with his hands on her shoulders. He was red-faced and panting. Momma patted Dad's quavering hands.

"Allister Grind was interested in me, and I was mildly interested in him. I thought he was the kind of man my parents expected me to marry, but when William died, I felt dead inside too. Then I ran away and landed in Bend."

Momma looked at me as she grasped Dad's hands.

"Just when I thought I'd not dare love anything or anyone again, this fool came into the diner and I found my one true love. My only regret was that I'd made a mistake with his fool friend a few days before."

Tears came in a steady stream for all of us.

Dad shuddered and jerked.

"My father thought I was a whore. And I proved him right. I had sex and got pregnant with Ben Twitchell's babies, but I didn't love Grind or Twitch. I loved Joseph, your dad. Still do, and will forever."

"Twitch?" My head swam. I was definitely out of my depths. I thought Twitch had shown Momma to Dad for him to have her. Why would Twitch be with her too?

Dad nodded and cried harder.

"Twitch is— It was his sperm, but no one has been a father to you more than Joseph. No one loves you and Becky and me more than your dad." Momma said the words with more conviction than her Bible thumping.

Dad raised his head and wiped his face on his sleeve, and when he came around in front of Momma and knelt beside her, she wiped at his tears and snot with the hem of her dress like he was a little boy. They looked at me. They probably wondered how much more ugliness I was capable of.

"I'm sorry," came out as a whisper, and I repeated it until I could see them nod and their eyes take me in. I swallowed and let their words sink into me, hoping the truth would feel less frightening than the lies. And it did. Twitch was my biological father, and although I loved him, he sure as hell wasn't my dad.

I was as awkward as a ballet dancer on ice, but I grabbed them and hugged and cried, snuffled and snotted, as I tried to climb in their arms and be alone with them, not letting an inch of me touch anything else in the world. And they hugged me back and cried and laughed.

There were choruses of "sorry" and "I love you" and reassurances that must have piled up inside of us over time only to come flooding out that day. I wished Becky were there to see us and pile on. We were a litter of puppies just glad to be with each other and part of each other.

CHAPTER TWENTY-FIVE
EXORCISM

Eventually, Kenny was released from jail. I heard he'd likely only get probation for his part in hiding his dad's death and body. He didn't come to our place the first day or the next. He had to bury his father the right way and tend to his mom, but after the funeral, Kenny came to the farm. It was totally awkward. There wasn't any guide to help our family go from having thought Kenny killed Becky to just thinking of him as the same old Kenny again.

Kenny knocked at the door and stood on the porch with his seed cap in his hand. Dad answered. Kenny said, "I'd like to see Little Man if that's okay with you."

Technically, Momma and Dad could have said no. They still had temporary custody of Little Man. Dad invited Kenny in and asked him if he had time to stay for lunch. This was Tyler speak for an apology. From then on, with Becky in the hospital for the foreseeable future, Kenny and Little Man became fixtures at our table.

Eventually the broken ribs he'd suffered in his come-to-Jesus with the steering wheel of his truck healed enough for him to help Dad mend fences, rotate stock, and tend the sheep and goats we pastured for Holcum. Stage two of a Tyler family apology was to put him to work.

Kenny told how he had convinced his mom to sell the pigs and seriously consider selling the whole farm. She was a strong wind away from getting herself a place in town close to a grocery store. She had not met many people in Bend. Momma said Kenny's mom's folks were from the Dakotas. and she had lived isolated by Mr. Hollister's wrath when he was well and by his cares when he was sick. Kenny said he hoped she could make a friend and have more of a life.

With tears and a strained voice, Kenny described how his dad had been a hard man, but that Kenny loved him and grieved his death. Kenny said that the old man had died in his bed peacefully. Kenny's momma had panicked that without his social security check along with hers, they wouldn't be able to keep the farm. Kenny said he should have known better, but he panicked too and buried his dad. He admitted he'd been afraid the dogs would desecrate the grave. He cried even harder as he confessed to shooting his dogs. He swore to us that he'd never hurt Becky and never would.

His words rolled off me. Becky was alive, so he hadn't killed her, but I knew he could be violent. He'd left bruises on me and on Becky. It would take more than his words to convince me he was fit to be Becky's husband or Little Man's dad.

Kenny bore his sadness and worry, but summoned energy for Little Man. I watched Kenny roughhouse with Little Man and hold his hands as he tried to stand and then walk. Sometimes, when Kenny took the boy, Little Man would put his arms out to me. I accepted every opportunity to supervise Kenny's time with his son. I wasn't ready to trust him with precious cargo. I stayed close and watchful.

Becky was locked in a psychiatric ward in St. Paul. I read books and articles Gerry brought me from the library. The history of mental health treatment read like a horror film. It gave me scary imaginings of shock treatment, leeches, bloodletting, and heavy tranquillizers. I had no idea what they were doing to her in the hospital. Despite Momma's calls, letters, and visits, the doctor wouldn't tell anyone anything. The doctor said that because Becky was an adult, she had rights to privacy, and because she was in a hospital, there was no imminent danger. Becky would need to sign a release for the doctor to talk with us. Becky refused.

I was frustrated. What had the doctor thought we were going to do with the information? We just wanted to know if Becky still talked crazy about Satan and when she could come home.

Momma, Dad, and I drove to the hospital every week on Sunday, but the hospital staff wouldn't tell us anything, and Becky wouldn't see us, only Kenny.

Suddenly, just before Easter, Becky was released. I suspected that the State's part of paying hospital costs ran out, and one look at our family didn't give the impression of deep pockets. The doctors and social workers nearly fell over themselves to give our family and Kenny information and instructions. They said Becky had schizophrenia and now that she finally agreed to take a medication, we were conscripted to "monitor" her medication compliance. If Becky became "religiously ideated and dangerous," we were "authorized" to bring Becky straight back to the hospital.

I didn't think a one of us understood what the doctors said. The prospect of making sure Becky took her medications seemed more daunting to me than drenching sheep or fixing stray cats. How do you prepare for someone's reentry back home from a psychiatric hospital stay? I had no clue. Momma, Dad, and Kenny seemed excited. I was scared shitless. Could she implode at any moment? Should we talk louder? Use more hand signals and shorter words?

Becky looked pretty much like herself. The bruises and cuts had healed. But she didn't have the energy I remembered. She talked and moved stiffly, but to my relief, she didn't talk about God or Satan right off. She didn't talk about the time she was missing or hospitalized. I was torn about whether I should hover around her or stay out of her hair. She made the decision for me. She had Little Man and Kenny to manage, a household to run. She got back to business, and her business was again none of mine. I sometimes spied on her with Momma's binoculars, and made up excuses to visit so I could get a look at Becky and make sure she was caring for Little Man.

Kenny called our house every day with reports. The postings were blessedly mundane.

"My girl cooked us all oatmeal for breakfast, and today, she and Little Man are doing laundry."

As the weight of worrying about Becky lifted, Momma, Dad, and I got back to living our own lives. Momma worked full-time at the diner. Dad called Twitch and told him that I could take the full-time job with him. I called the admissions department at college and asked for the paperwork to apply again. And with my parents' permission and reluctance, I asked for student loan applications. I saw Charity when I could, but I kept one eye peeled in case Little Man needed me to step in.

At first, Becky visited the farm every day, or every other day, and seemed herself mostly. Occasionally, she let her anger slip. She berated Dad and Twitch for taking her to a hospital, and she accused Momma and me of abandoning her there for days on end. Becky's anger made sense to me in one way. No one likes a cage, and mommas certainly don't like being separated from their babies, but we hadn't abandoned her. She'd left us without an explanation when she got sick, and when she was getting well she had refused to let us have a part in her treatment at the hospital.

I could only imagine how it irked Becky seeing how comfortable Little Man had become in my arms and the arms of Momma and Dad. I don't know if she knew about Kenny having called the house with daily reports. I didn't see any new bruises and couldn't tell anything from his reports. Once Becky stopped visiting our place as regularly, it was pretty tough to know what was going on with her.

One day Kenny said, "My girl is back to her old self. She's got what's left of the farm running like a clock. I can't tell she was even in the hospital." Another day he said, "Boy, you should see the energy she has. Everything is spic-and-span and then some. She's even cleaning at night."

Before I could ask her why in the hell she was cleaning at night, Becky stopped visiting with us period. She offered no explanation or excuse. When she came over at all it was to drop off Little Man. She mumbled about things she had to do. Kenny's calls to the house decreased and changed too.

"My girl is having a quiet day today, resting," Kenny told me. "Probably from all the work she did last week. I've got the boy with me. May have to drop him off at your place later so I can get some work done."

Another day, I was startled awake before dawn. Kenny's booming voice assaulted the air a moment after the screen door slammed behind him. Dad was the only one fully dressed and conscious. Momma was in the bathroom. Kenny had Little Man with him and needed someone to watch him so he could haul the remaining pigs to a slaughterhouse in St. Wendell and get back and clean his empty barns.

"It's a good day for reading your Bible," Kenny said. "Hard to argue with a woman on that, although I wish she'd start picking up again."

I poked my head out from my bedroom. "Is Becky going loony again with her God talk? Is she taking her medications? The doctor said—"

"I heard the doctor the same as you," Kenny snapped at me.

"Well?"

"Just watch Little Man today so I can get those barns cleaned, please." He let the screen door slam again on his way out, got in his truck, and raced from the yard. It went on like that for another week. Becky didn't come over, and if she was at home, she didn't answer the door or phone when I called. Kenny just appeared and dropped off Little Man each morning like we should be waiting to take care of him and had nothing else to do. Then he retrieved him each afternoon. It wasn't that any of us minded taking care of Little Man. We were in love with him, but it made us wonder what Becky was doing that she'd give up so much time with her son.

Easter weekend Kenny called in a fit.

"She doesn't change her clothes anymore or cook or clean, or any of the other stuff we used to do together that is none of your business, Lorraine. She just reads that Bible and prays."

"I'll talk to her. Put her on the phone." There was a long silence, but I could hear Kenny still breathing into the phone. "Kenny, put Becky on the phone and I'll talk to her."

"I can't. She, um . . ."

"Okay, I'll come over there and talk to her."

"You can't!" Kenny said. "She's gone. Shit! Shit! Shit! She took her Bible and she took Little Man." There was empty air on the phone until Kenny came clean. "She didn't take her pills."

"What do you mean? She didn't take them with her when she left?"

"No, goddamn it. She didn't take them at all. The bottle is here, I counted them, and there's not but two missing."

"Shit." I couldn't believe he hadn't watched her better.

"I'm scared, Lorraine. We've got to find her before she does something."

CHAPTER TWENTY-SIX
ATONEMENT

I slammed the phone down. *The fool.* It was easy to blame him at first. The idiot should have watched Becky closer, but I also felt convicted in my heart. I wanted it both ways. I wanted Becky to be better, but I didn't want to have to work for that too. I guessed I could have watched Becky more closely and maybe even spied on her medications. Now Becky had run off again, and this time she had Little Man with her.

I was alone and frantic with worry. Momma and Dad weren't home. Twitch wasn't at his office. Charity was under house arrest at her place and hadn't had phone privileges since Grind found out about we'd been sneaking out to be together. Jolene was at college. Out of ideas and allies, I remembered that Gerry Narrows had helped me before.

"No, she's not at my place, but I know where she is," Gerry said. "I saw her drive that poor excuse for a truck into your west pasture about an hour ago. She had the boy with her. I thought she was probably showing Little Man the sheep and goats. Is everything okay?"

"I hope so. Talk to you later. Thanks, Gerry."

I scribbled a note to Momma and Dad to call Kenny and come to the west pasture. Becky was in trouble.

The quickest route to the west pasture was through the yard, over the fence, and over a hill through the woods. It was the same route I'd walked with Charity the winter we'd met. The few beef cattle Dad kept had trampled trails through the grasses and brush. Maples, oaks, and quaking aspen crowded the sky with their new spring leaves.

Once I crested the hill, I heard Becky before I saw her. She was about fifty feet below me where the hill petered out and a fence line separated the woods from the hay fields. I watched and listened. Becky was pacing and praying.

Becky's hair looked ratted and unwashed. She wore the same dress she'd worn the last time she'd visited the farm. Before I could yell about Becky's dumbass decision to not take medications, and her dumber-ass decision to take Little Man without telling anybody where she was going, I saw that Becky held a knife.

I stopped in my tracks. The sun glinted off the long blade as Becky gestured with it and talked out loud.

"I am here, Lord. You have tested me. Here I am." She paced and chanted, and stooped to pick up a stick, adding it to a pile of wood. "The sacrifice must be blameless."

I scanned the area for Little Man. He was on a blanket on the ground, motionless beside the growing stack of wood. I trotted toward them.

"Becky."

"Lord," Becky said into the sky, "I have brought you a blameless lamb."

"Becky!" I edged closer but worried I'd spook her.

"Lord, I have a sacrifice for you: my son."

Shit, goddamn it, holy Christ. She was out of her head again, and this time she was thinking of hurting Little Man.

"Becky, don't do this."

Becky jerked around and looked at me. "Lorraine, don't worry, my sister. God is going to bless you too. Our children will be as plentiful as the stars. We will own the cities."

With that proclamation, she actually twirled and raised her hands in the air. Her foot grazed Little Man, and he stirred.

He was alive. Oh God. I couldn't bear the thought of losing him.

"Becky, you stopped your medicine."

"I had to Lorraine. I couldn't hear His voice. God stopped talking to me."

She bent down and stroked Little Man's cheek. He turned on his belly, sucked his thumb, and nuzzled into the blanket, napping.

There was still twenty feet of ground between Becky and me physically, and miles between us in understanding.

I said, "God doesn't want you to sacrifice Little Man."

"How do you know what God wants Lorraine? Do you hear his voice? You don't even believe." She paced more quickly and took furtive glances at me.

If it weren't for the knife she held and her close proximity to Little Man, I would have run, tackled her, and held her down until somebody came to help. I stalled and tried to get closer to her.

"You're right, Becky. I didn't believe, but I do now." I inched closer. "I believed since that first day I saw you and Little Man together. Remember? You said, 'Look what love has made.'" Another inch. "I believe because I met Charity, and she is kind and beautiful and loving and she believes in God."

"Don't bring up your debauchery to me, Lorraine." Becky glared.

Shit! Why'd I bring up Charity? I stood frozen and floundered for words and wisdom. "What about Momma? I believe in God because Momma does even though her little brother died in a horrible accident and she's blamed herself all these years. Still she loves us."

"I was chosen, not you. God chose me. You all want me to take those pills so I'd be just the same as you. I'm not the same as you. I am blessed. God speaks to me." Becky put her hands to the side of her head and nearly cut off her right ear.

"Just calm down. Let's talk this through." I came closer while Becky looked off in another direction.

Becky's head snapped up like she was being called from the clouds.

"I am here, Lord. You have tested me, but I have passed," she said, and without warning, she bent down and lifted a red metal gas can that I hadn't even seen. The lid was off. She took the can with both her hands while still holding the knife, and she splashed gas on the woodpile.

"Oh God, Becky, you can't do this. God doesn't want you to kill Little Man."

"He is blameless before God, a perfect sacrifice." She looked at Little Man on the blanket.

What could I do, what could I do? She wanted to sacrifice Little Man like he was a dumb sheep. Sheep. Holcum's sheep! "Becky, use one of the sheep."

"What?"

"There are blameless sheep right here in this pasture. I'll help you catch one."

"I am being tested like Abraham."

"Yes, and you passed like Abraham. Just like Abraham." It was one of the few Old Testament stories I remembered, because it was so creepy.

"You passed, Becky. Like Abraham you were willing to sacrifice your only son. Becky, remember the rest of the story?"

"Genesis 22: 'God called Abraham, and Abraham called back, "Here I am,"'" Becky said.

"But God stopped Abraham before Abraham sacrificed Isaac. God sent an angel."

"You're no angel of the Lord, Lorraine," she said.

"You're right, Becky. I'm no angel, but I can catch sheep. Remember after the angel told Abraham to stop, he caught a ram in the thicket for Abraham to use as a sacrifice?"

I could tell my words were conflicting with the voices in Becky's head. Becky furrowed her brow and grabbed her head again. Then she turned toward Little Man and leaned over.

I lunged forward and pushed Becky down. The fall jarred the knife from her hand. She crawled on the ground to retrieve it. I swept Little Man up, and flat out ran. Becky yelled for me to stop and bring her lamb back to her.

Little Man's head bobbed against my shoulder as I carried him through the pasture and up the hill. He awakened and smiled at me like it was the most normal thing in the world for me to be running through the woods with him. I guessed it was.

I stopped at the top of the hill. Becky hadn't followed me. She watched me and lifted her hand—the one with the knife—and gave a wave.

I looked toward the farm and saw Momma, Dad, and Kenny in the yard. I yelled to them and motioned for them to come. I put Little Man on his wobbly feet next to a tree facing away from Becky, and in view of his dad and grandparents.

"Little Man, you wait right here. Daddy, Grandma, and Grandpa are coming." The little bugger lowered to his knees and crawled toward his grandparents and dad.

In the time it'd taken for me to position Little Man, Becky had started the wood altar on fire. The fire *whoosh*ed, lapping at the gasoline and dry wood. I called to Becky, but she looked up to the sky like it was God who was screaming her name and telling her what to do.

Becky spoke into the air, "I know he'd be better. I have sinned. I'm not perfect. I'm not enough, but take me, take me!" She held the gas can above her head. She dumped the gasoline that was left over her head and onto her clothes.

I ran to her. I wasn't fast enough.

Becky plunged the knife into her belly and dropped into the flames.

I'd failed. A second *whoosh* pierced the air, followed by yelling. Dad and Kenny had reached the top of the hill. Like me, they were running full out toward the fire as Becky's strangled screams shrilled from the fire and smoke below.

I tried to save Becky. Dad, Kenny, and I all tried to save her, pull her from the flames. Fire licked at my hands, and I heard the crackle of hair singeing as I grabbed Becky. I gripped her ankles. The skin felt like warm dough.

Kenny reached into the flames to help me. We dragged Becky out and away from the fire. Dad snuffed out Becky's burning clothes with the same blanket that Little Man had napped on. When he pulled it away, patches of Becky's scorched skin and clothes clung to the cloth. She was charred and bleeding. She was no longer my sister, Kenny's wife, or Dad's daughter.

She was dead.

I hoped she was with God.

Dad pulled Becky farther from the fire.

Kenny clung to her and cried, "No, no, no!"

I looked at Dad. He said stuff but I couldn't register his words, only the sound of the fire, crackling and creeping over the dried ground. The smoke and stench of burned gas and wood and flesh clogged my nose. My eyes burned no matter how many tears flooded them.

Time stood still and sped by. It felt like everything happened in an instant, and it also felt endless. When Sheriff Scrogrum showed up, he yammered something about the pasture on fire and that he'd radioed for a fire truck.

Dad put his hand on Kenny's shoulder and put out his arms. Kenny let Dad gather Becky up into his arms and carry her toward the sheriff's cruiser at the edge of the field next to Kenny's truck.

"I don't want her momma seeing her like this. She's got Little Man, and she's coming here with the car. We got to get Becky out of here," Dad said. The blanket trailed behind them like the bloodied train of a bridal dress.

"Put her in the car, Joseph. I'll direct the fire fighters when they come," the sheriff said. "We'll save your land."

"Let it burn!" Dad yelled over his shoulder.

A quarter of the west pasture was ablaze by the time the volunteer firefighters arrived. They didn't let the rest of it burn, of course. Putting out that fire was the only thing they could do for our family. Sheriff Scrogrum shushed them with just a look when they started asking questions about Becky.

Dad placed Becky's body in the back of the sheriff's cruiser and drove her away. I was left behind to face Momma. She drove up in the station wagon and took the spot Dad had just vacated. I was relieved and saddened to my core to see Little Man was with Momma. She left Little Man in his car seat. I could see his head bobbing up from the backseat.

How could I possibly tell Momma that Becky was dead? I understood all the stammering and prevaricating adults used when they tried to say bad news.

"Oh, Momma. She's dead. Becky's dead."

Momma looked back and forth between me and the fire and chaos.

"Dad took her in the sheriff's car, but she's dead, Momma. Becky's dead."

"No, you're wrong. That just can't be."

I couldn't say it again. I shook my head and regarded Momma.

Momma spun on her heels and headed back to the car. I ran after her and got in the backseat with Little Man. I held his clean hand in my soot-covered, burned hands. At first, Momma drove like she was trying to catch up with Dad, and then she just pulled the car to the shoulder, put her head against the steering wheel, and sobbed.

CHAPTER TWENTY-SEVEN
RECONCILIATION

If anyone had asked me, I would have said that grief was a marathon, but funerals were a sprint. Becky died one day, and Momma, Dad, and Kenny met with a funeral director the following day. Our community, friends, and gawkers came to the reviewal and visitation at the funeral home the day after that. The funeral director used the word "reviewal," but there was no open casket, not that those of us who'd seen her burned up could ever forgot what she looked like. Her graduation picture was propped on the closed casket, mocking us with how beautiful she'd been before.

Twitch told me that the coroner said Becky had been dead from the stab wound before she ever hit the flames. I knew differently, but I appreciated Twitch's attempt to ease my pain and imagination. To return the favor, I never told him how Dad, Kenny, and I had heard Becky's screams from the flames.

I marched along like a good soldier, helped Momma pick music and flowers, and recruited pallbearers and goulash makers. Jolene came home from college and accompanied Charity to my house each day. They made me and my folks eat and decide things. I was grateful that Pastor Grind allowed his daughters to be in the company of the queer Tyler girl.

Momma selected a picture and verse to put on Becky's funeral program. Becky's short life had left white space, a brief list of who had preceded her in death, and a longer list of who had survived.

The funeral was the day after the reviewal. The church choir sang, and a group of high school girls played their flutes. Pastor Grind presided over the funeral. He was quiet and kind in the way he spoke about Becky and her brief life. He pulled out familiar scriptures and songs. Pastor Grind stumbled to explain what not a one of us believed could be explained. Momma clutched a hymnal. I hoped she'd throw it at his head if he dared quote anything about Abraham or sacrifice. I crushed into the same pew as Momma, Dad, Twitch, Kenny, Little Man, Jolene, and Charity. It was only their shoulders on either side of me that kept me upright. Becky was buried near the edge of the farm at Bear Head Cemetery.

After the internment, Twitch asked me to ride back to the church with him. I wasn't sure I wanted to. I figured it meant we'd have to talk about something besides animals and what ails them. We had worked side by side for weeks since I learned he was my biological father, but neither of us had said anything about it to the other.

"I don't mind missing the goulash and Jell-O if you don't," he said.

"No, I don't mind." We stood on the artificial turf that skirted the area a few yards back from Becky's grave. The grave-digging crew milled about nearby—just a hole to fill in and then the crew could get back to the living. I resented them. Why were they so eager to cover Becky up? I hated them for their job, but couldn't have dropped a teaspoon of dirt into that hole myself.

"So, now you know about me and your momma."

"Have you always known?"

"Yeah. Your momma told your dad the truth right away. God, how I wanted to tell you."

"Is that why you've been taking me places and teaching me about animals?"

"No. Your dad and I were and are best friends. I would've been around getting to know you anyway. Of course, I was interested because you girls were my blood, but I didn't have any illusions about taking over raising you. Joseph and Peggy are your parents."

He put his hand on my back and steered me toward his Jeep.

"I kept asking you to go places and teaching you about animals because I liked you. I love you, Lorraine. I loved Becky too, but she was a bit harder to get close to."

"Becky could be kind of prickly sometimes."

"You got to understand that I wanted to help you girls more. I got a few dollars, but your folks were set on providing for you girls themselves. I don't know if Becky dying will jerk them out of that rut or not."

I had a head full of questions I wanted to ask him, but only braved asking two of the most pressing.

"Can I still work for you and save for school?"

"Of course you can," Twitch said, and hugged me. It was one of those A-frame–type hugs that don't allow for much body contact.

It was a start. I buried my face in the front of Twitch's shirt and asked him the second question.

"Am I going to get sick too? Is this like some of those illnesses that if one of the litter gets it, they all do?"

"No, honey. It's not bacteria or something like that."

Before Twitch escaped into the Jeep, I grabbed him around the shoulders and gave him the hug he should have started that day and in the thousands of days since I was a kid. I didn't know if I totally believed him that I was safe from the sickness Becky had, but I knew my momma and dad would be there, and I knew Twitch would be there to guide me as much as his science and love would let him.

Grief was a marathon.

None of us had trained.

We lacked endurance, wind capacity, and even proper shoes. Most nights I feared sleep because of nightmares of Becky in the fire. It wasn't that I didn't think about it during the day, but at night, if sleep caught me, I couldn't get away from the pictures, sounds, and smells. I didn't ask Dad or Kenny if they were having the same problem, in case they weren't. I didn't want to start it for them.

I put one foot in front of the other and kept moving. Momma, Dad, and Kenny did the same, I supposed. Caring for Little Man helped. I went through the motions of living a life if only for the fact that I needed to do my part in taking care of Becky's son. The animals on the farm and in Twitch's vet practice made demands, oblivious to my desire to cocoon until the memories faded and hurt less.

Once spring passed into summer, Momma rose up like the humidity and took matters into her own hands. For once, I was glad that Momma took control. She started the healing. As usual, she used food. She began cooking again.

She started off easy and made fried chicken. She took the pudgy drumsticks and thighs, dipped them in milk, coated them in bread crumbs, and browned them in Crisco oil until they looked like something kissed by the sun. She cooked fresh garden vegetables—not from our garden, we hadn't planted a thing that year. Momma used vegetables from Gerry and other neighbors who dropped things off, not knowing what more they could do.

Momma took the onions, carrots, and other produce and nestled them beside pork roasts and beef roasts. She put them adrift in chicken broth and cream sauces. She baked bread, cinnamon rolls, caramel rolls, and molasses buns. She stirred lump-free brown gravies and added a titch of coffee if the color wasn't deep enough. She fed Dad and me, and Little Man and Kenny when they stayed for dinner.

Eventually, the days didn't seem so pointless. Momma's appetite and opinionated attitude returned. Dad's laughter escaped without the look of self-conscious guilt. Neighbors and friends visited. Pastor and Mrs. Grind, Jolene and Charity, Twitch, and Gerry came often. Talking soon overtook the silences. Language about Becky settled into past tense and airbrushed reminiscence.

Becky would not be resurrected by penance from me or anyone else. Becky was dead.

CHAPTER TWENTY-EIGHT
FORGIVENESS

June passed. I turned nineteen, but couldn't really imagine celebrating. Becky's absence was still too glaring. Momma made a cake, red velvet with cream cheese frosting, Becky's and my favorite. Jolene bought me a bird field guide, and Charity made a pencil sketch of me holding Little Man.

Then in late July, just after Little Man's first birthday, I told Momma I couldn't grieve Becky anymore.

"I'll always remember her, Momma, but I can't sit under the weight of her absence. I have to live my life."

If Momma thought me selfish, she didn't say it or write it in her notebook. Momma gave the signal that it was time to move on with other parts of life. Even though Momma was scared, she made up her mind to go to Clearmont to see her mother.

"What if she doesn't know me?" Momma asked. "What if she won't talk to me? What if I wasted my chance?"

"What momma wouldn't be thrilled to see her child again?" I said.

Momma even let me drive.

The station wagon was still badly dented from Momma's demolition derby in Kenny's yard. The passenger door didn't open, so now our car matched our truck. Momma slid into the passenger seat from the driver's side of the car. Her feet tapped the floorboards, and she fidgeted in the passenger seat to the point of getting abrasions from her seat belt. She clutched the Jesus bar the whole way to Clearmont.

When Momma and I arrived, the nursing home was bustling with activity. A bingo game had broken out in the lunchroom about the same time as somebody had left the door open to the aviary. Diamond doves and canaries flew through the TV lounge to the nurses' station, to the lunchroom, and back to the aviary where they thumped the glass in attempts to return to their nests.

Sassy, the official Clearmont Home for the Aged cat, chased through the halls hunting exotic birds. Old people who hadn't raised their hands above their heads in years swatted at dive-bombing, pastel-colored birds. Momma and I found Grandma lying motionless on her bed in her room.

"Oh God, she's already dead," Momma said.

Grandma rose up. "Who's dead?"

"Mom?" Momma moved slowly toward her mother.

"Margaret?" Grandma lay down again, but she turned her head and looked at Momma. "You've gotten fat."

Normally, those would have been fighting words. I waited for Momma to lash out and maybe leave, but Momma didn't flare up. It was like she was little—young inside. She toddled to Grandma, pulled a chair close to the bed, and sat.

I watched and actually prayed from the doorway. Momma had lost Becky. I hoped that she could salvage her relationship with Grandma.

"Mom, my baby died too. I know how you hurt when William died. Now, I know." Momma wrung her hands.

Grandma's mind was a worn transmission. It slipped and stalled between present and past like she was trying to rock a car out of a rut in the snow.

"Oh, you poor dear," she said. "No parent should ever have to go through that. It's just not natural to see your child die before you." She closed her eyes. "Of course it happened to me. It wasn't so uncommon then, farm accidents, but still you think that when you get them past that baby time that they should just live and grow up."

Grandma sat up in bed, swung her legs to the floor, shifted her mind gears into drive, and pressed the accelerator.

"Margaret, how are your girls?"

Momma moved with Grandma's mind like her hand was on the same gearshift.

"I have the best girls, Mom. You'd be so proud. They graduated top of their class—both scholarship winners. Lorraine is right here with me." Momma waved me over closer to Grandma.

"Yes, of course. She's a pretty girl." Grandma squinted and looked past us to the doorway. "And where's that Rebecca?"

"Oh Mom, my Becky died."

"I'm so sorry. That's the hardest thing. I don't know how to soothe your heart. Just don't make the mistake I made. Love the children you have left like they could be gone tomorrow."

Grandma rocked and hummed. "I lost a child, a son. Take it from this old woman, I know. You've got to hold the babies you have left— the ones that died don't need you no more. The live ones need you."

That did it. I thought I would fall over. Momma quaked and spilled. Her individual tears were not distinguishable in the continuous stream down her face.

Grandma looked at me and bent forward.

"What's your name, honey? Are you the new aid? You look so much like my Margaret. She's a nurse." Her mind seemed to slip again and she said, "Where'd I put that paper?"

She rummaged through the three drawers in her nightstand, searched her basket of knitting, and then pulled a wrinkled paper out of the bosom of her slip.

"Gotcha. Here it is, Margaret." She handed the paper to me. The paper had once been a placemat. On one side knives, folks, and spoons danced with salt and pepper shakers. The other side had a hand-drawn map of a farmstead—house, barn, grain silo, chicken coop, well house. I smoothed the paper out on top of the wheeled table that flanked Grandma's bed.

"That's our home farm." Momma ran her hand over the crude drawing.

"Margaret." This time Grandma looked at Momma. "You really should go out there and get that nest egg we saved for you. Be a nurse. Get your white cap."

Grandma pivoted, put her feet on the bed, and closed her eyes. Her mouth fell open moments later and she let out a snuffly s nore. Her troubled mind must have eased into park.

I followed the blacktop out of Clearmont at Momma's instructions. As far as I was concerned we were headed in the wrong direction. I no more believed that nest egg existed than I believed in the Easter bunny.

The paved road gave way to a rutted gravel road. The dust rose and choked me until I closed the window and vents. What seemed like a ditch turned out to be an overgrown driveway. Thigh-high grasses and bushes combed the undercarriage of the station wagon, and woody branches scratched the windows and doors. Just beyond a windbreak of scrubby pine trees stood what remained of the farm where Momma had grown up.

The house, a saltbox structure, had lost its paint, and all the windows were broken out. The grain silo had collapsed upon itself into rubble. The chicken coop leaned west and the well house listed east like they were stooping to hear what the other had whispered.

The barn still stood. Its windows were gone, giving it the look of a vacant face. I parked as close to it as I dared. The barn appeared like it could collapse any moment.

"We don't have a shovel," Momma said.

"Don't tell me you believe that nest egg is still here?"

"What do we have to lose in checking? She drew us a map." She turned the map in her hand. "I know this barn. We are right here. The nest egg is in the northwest corner of the barn." She pointed and started to move toward the barn.

"I'm not going in there. That barn is ready to fall down."

"It's not that old. It just looks old because no one has used it or taken care of it for years. Besides, there might be money for college in there."

I crossed my arms over my chest and refused to look at Momma. "I'm working for Twitch and taking out a small student loan."

"Hard to know what animals are in those weeds and the barn," Momma said.

"Okay. I'll go with you, but I don't believe there's any money." I grabbed the flashlight from the glove box and went around to the back of the wagon to get the tire iron.

"Good, Lorraine. If we see snakes or rats you can swat them with that."

"I'm not killing anything. This is to dig up that money."

We picked our way through the long grass, burdocks, and thistles. Cicadas whined. The barn door no longer hung on its track. I used the tire iron to pry it open. The wood shredded like dry turkey breast, but enough of it held together so that I could lever it open and get through. I leaned against it from the inside and created a gap large enough for Momma. If Momma got any slivers or cuts, she didn't complain.

Light filtered through the windows on either end of the barn, but not enough to help me know where to step or see what animals were skittering along the floor and in the haymow above.

I squeezed the rubber grip of the flashlight and turned it on. Momma took my arm and pointed in the direction of what I assumed was the northwest corner of the barn, but looked like a black hole in space.

Old straw crunched under my feet. Barn swallows abandoned their nests and flew out the glassless windows as Momma and I made our way through the barn. There was dried manure a foot, foot and a half deep in some places. I wondered how old the shit was. Had my grandpa left it like this, or was I walking on the remnants of work other farmers had failed to do?

Momma looked around her. She touched the wooden beams. "My dad and his dad built this barn. Can you picture men straddled on the rafters, first nailing roof boards, then tar paper to the roof and later shingling it? Some of the haymow boards were nailed in place by me once I was strong enough to swing the ten-ounce hammer Dad gave me for the job. I remember trying my first cigarette in that haymow. It's a wonder I didn't burn the place down."

The northwest corner of the barn had a manger that had kept the hay up off the floor. Momma held the flashlight while I pulled and pried the rotted boards away. I kicked stale, decomposing hay out of the corner until I got to concrete.

Momma shined the flashlight down on the floor.

"Look under here," she said. The light started to flicker like the batteries were giving out. She slapped the flashlight against her hand, and it worked again. I knelt and swept debris away until I reached the cement floor. I felt along the floor for cracks in the cement. I found a fault line just as the light failed again.

"Goddamn it!"

Momma's swearing scared me more than the darkness. I rose up and banged my head on a board. I knelt again and passed my hands over the cement like I was reading a braille holy book. "I found a crack."

"Well?" Momma asked.

"Do you want me to try to pry up the pieces of concrete here in the dark? Or should we go and come back with a new light?"

"I'm tired of waiting. Try to open that hole."

I felt around for the tire iron. I located the crack again and put the beveled end of the tire iron on top of the opening. I pressed down and rocked the tool. The compromised concrete powdered against the steel and the edge of the tire iron sunk. I levered the loose pieces away. After I'd opened an area just slightly larger than a dinner plate, I put my hands in the dirt below and dug.

The sand and gravel felt cold and wet. It gave way more easily than I'd expected. I hadn't been digging very long when I hit something hard. It felt and sounded like metal when I tapped against it with my fingernails. I cursed the useless flashlight and the irresponsible family that had left it in the car with dead batteries.

"What would Grandma and Grandpa have buried it in?"

"I don't know." Momma lowered herself to her knees. There was no way Momma could get back to her feet without a tractor and logging chain, especially if there was the added weight of disappointment if we didn't find the nest egg.

"It's a can—probably a coffee can." She put her hands in the hole and fingered the thing I had found.

We both dug like possessed pocket gophers. We got the can loose and held it between us there in the dark.

"Can you lead us out of this place?" I asked Momma.

"I can."

I took the can, put it on the floor, and stood up. I helped Momma to her feet. As I reached for the can and the tire iron, the barn boards creaked and shifted.

I turned to Momma. "That seems about right. I'm going to be crushed just before possibly finding enough money for me to go to college."

Momma led the way. I was at her hip. We inched along the barn floor as the walls below the gambrel roof moaned. When we found the door where we'd come in, Momma pushed the door and made an opening for me. I went through and pulled the door open enough for Momma to pass through.

Spiderwebs and straw netted Momma's hair, mud and dust caked her hands and knees, and I noticed for the first time that Momma was a beautiful woman. I had probably entertained those thoughts years before, but no time recently. She had been a big aggravation and obstacle to me—nothing beautiful. But there she was, not yet forty and her losses would have wizened anyone, but she was still young and beautiful.

"Let's open this can, Momma."

The lid had rusted and adhered to the can. I used my jackknife blade to pry around the edges, but it wouldn't budge. I was ready to tear at it with my teeth when Momma found a good use for that dead flashlight. She beat on the can, and it separated at the seams.

Inside was a bundle wrapped in wax paper. Momma placed the bundle on the car hood and fumbled with the paper.

Momma jerked and gasped. There was her high school diploma, yellowed but legible.

"I ran away," she said. "I thought I made graduation, but I never saw my diploma to know for sure." Tears streamed from her eyes. Just that piece of paper would probably have been enough, but there was more. There were William's and Momma's birth certificates. Momma took each document into her hands, examined it, and handed it to me.

"Look here, Lorraine." She handed me a black-and-white photograph. The back of the photo read, *County Fair 19__, Michael, Aggie, Margaret, and William.*

"We had our family picture taken at the fair. I was five, and William was a baby." Momma petted the photo like she could touch her brother and dad.

The last thing in the bundle were woolen socks.

Shit.

My heart fell.

Grandma's idea of a college nest egg was a few documents and equipment for warm feet. Momma tossed the socks to me.

"There you go, daughter." She grinned at me.

"Great. Just what I need is wool socks."

"That's just one sock," Momma said. "Look inside."

I unrolled the sock, found the opening, and reached inside.

CHAPTER TWENTY-NINE
SURRENDER

I had money for college.

It wasn't the McGerber scholarship. That money wasn't right for our family anyway. It certainly wasn't right for me. There were too many strings attached to money from a holy man, too many expectations of what it meant to love God.

The money I did have had been earned by my grandparents. The nest egg was real. Momma gave me the money that would have been hers if she hadn't gotten pregnant with Becky and me. This was what I had wanted. I finally had an immediate way out, so why hadn't I packed my bags? I couldn't answer my own question. I made like I could and pulled my duffel from under my bed with an idea that I would begin packing.

I held the money in my hands. The bills were soft and wrinkled from years in a woolen sock, in a coffee can buried under the cracked cement of Grandma and Grandpa's barn. The money smelled musty and sour. I imagined that a forensic scientist—maybe one of those CSI folks—could have looked at the bills under a microscope and seen my grandparents' sweat-smeared fingerprints on them. I counted them again, one hundred hundred-dollar bills, enough to build a small house at the time they'd first been put in the steel can. They didn't use it for themselves. They'd put it in a can for their children and covered it with cement—maybe so they wouldn't change their mind. Then they'd told the story to their children. One child died, and it took a lifetime for the other child to believe she had the right to take what was promised.

Momma would let me go now. Momma's power was lost, or perhaps surrendered as if all the time it had been sustained through secrets, and maybe Becky. Becky was gone, and I could go too.

A towhead peeked around the doorway at me. Grinning and smeared with cookie crumbs, Little Man came into my room. He walked and wobbled with his hands outstretched to catch the wall or anything he could reach for balance. Then he just fell to his diapered bottom and crawled the rest of the way.

He grasped my jean legs. I picked him up into my arms and smelled his creamy neck. He clapped his pudgy hands on each side of my cheeks and gave me a slobbery kiss.

"You've been eating peanut butter cookies."

Little Man let one hand slide down and looped it around my neck. He put his thumb in his mouth, but not before he pointed out the door. I knew what he wanted. He wanted to catch some squirrels, which was just his way of saying he wanted to be with me. Just that quickly, I knew what I wanted too, and it wasn't the money meant for Momma. It wasn't leaving Bend on someone else's money, sweat, or benevolence. I wanted to make my own way, and I knew I could.

I put the money back in my pocket and left the duffel.

A person could register for school and not even be the person who was going to take the classes. A person could do that if they had the money to pay for the school, the student's personal information, and a good friend, like a librarian. Gerry took Momma's birth certificate, high school diploma, and the ten thousand dollars, and helped me register Momma in a nursing program at the area vocational technical college. I didn't tell Momma until it was said and done and Momma had been accepted. I handed Momma a class schedule and a backpack filled with textbooks.

"Momma, your folks intended for you to have that nest egg. I'm sorry it took so long for you to get it. I hope you will use it now."

Momma looked at Dad and back again at me. "No. I can't."

"Yes, you can. I'm going to work full-time with Twitch and take out some loans for college."

Momma was bug-eyed and dizzy for a moment before taking me into her arms and squeezing the breath out of me. I wouldn't have moved for anything. Momma suddenly pulled back and a panicked expression cut her face.

"What about Little Man? Kenny isn't going to be able to take care of him without help."

"I'm going to stay home and take care of Little Man, until I leave for college in January," I said. "I don't want to let the drooling critter go just yet. Besides, it'll take me until then to get these fools trained to watch him when I'm gone."

Momma could find a loophole in every plan and wouldn't let me off the hook too quickly. "What about the money I make at the diner? Our family needs me to work."

For once I was prepared for Momma's arguments. "Dad and Kenny both are taking jobs from Twitch. Dad's going to run the lumberyard, and he indentured Kenny there too as long as Kenny agrees to get his GED. There'll be money enough for us to get by."

Dad stepped up. He put his arm around Momma's shoulders.

"Peggy, honey, you got to just worry about yourself this time. You go to school. I'll take care of things here."

Momma's head fell onto his shoulder. "I know you'll fill this yard with junk everyday I'm gone."

"Yep, I probably will."

"And you'll probably feed Little Man candy and boxed dinners."

"Yep, that sounds like me."

"You'll probably let Lorraine run around with Charity and give Pastor Grind a stroke."

"Yep, I think that Charity is a nice girl, and I trust Lorraine. The fact that it chaffs Grind only encourages me."

They both laughed and snuggled against each other. As much as I wanted to share the hug, I left them to themselves.

"Can you keep working with Kenny after all that's happened?" Momma asked.

"Hell, not only can I work with him, I told him he should move into the upstairs and help me finish off those rooms for him and Little Man. We'll get Kenny on the right track," Dad said.

"Little Man can keep living with us?" Momma put her hand to her mouth and started crying. "It would be good to have that boy around."

CHAPTER THIRTY
RAPTURE

I still hadn't told Charity about my old fears that she was actually my half sister. It all seemed like a lifetime ago in some ways. In other ways, it was still fresh and achy. I waited for a private moment, called Charity, and hoped to collect the rest of my college good luck gift even if I wasn't going to college quite yet.

"Hey, Charity. Maybe if you're free tonight, I could come see you. I don't think I properly thanked you for that camisole you made for me."

There was silence on the line.

"If you liked the camisole, wait until you read the panties. Be here at 7 p.m." Charity hung up.

Charity was right about the panties, of course. I never thought of underwear as a great read, but I learned that when they were worn by someone you loved, and it was the first time you'd ever touched that person without clothes or reservations, then underpants were a fascinating read. Charity's deserved the Pulitzer Prize.

I traced over the words with my fingers.

"Hold still. This is small print. How am I supposed to read what you've written here if you keep wiggling like that?"

"I've never known you to be such a slow reader." Charity squirmed as I read.

Love, caress, rosebud lips, tongue, lick.

"What's here below this seam? I just can't quite read it."

Charity lifted her knees and dropped her legs apart. I nibbled Charity's thighs as I moved closer to read: *Only you know me.*

I looked up into Charity's face, smiled, and climbed Charity's body until I covered the length of her. Our legs braided together and

Charity's epic poem rested warm and damp against my upper thigh. I kissed her. "I have wanted to make love to you since the first time I saw you. But I don't really know what to do exactly."

Charity took my face in her hands. "Making love starts with good kissing, and you are a fabulous kisser, Lorraine Tyler. From kissing it's just improvisation, and the moves come pretty natural." She kissed me again. "The most difficult part—tell me if you find this isn't true—the hard part is that so much of your body wants to be touched all at once. You're going to wish for more hands and mouths and time. Remember, we have time and every inch of you will get attention."

She kept her word. Several times.

CHAPTER THIRTY-ONE
RESURRECTION

Dad, Kenny, Little Man, Charity, and I saw Momma off to school on her first day. I wished Becky could have been there to see it and do something with Momma's hair. Momma wore her blue dress, but instead of her Bible she toted a backpack of nursing books.

Dad had packed Momma a lunch. I'd seen him put love notes in with the sandwich, pudding pack, and fruit cocktail.

Momma got in the station wagon. Through her open window she handed me her notebook.

"Open it," she said.

It was empty. All the pages were blank. I handed it back to her. She scribbled something on a page, folded the paper, and handed it to me.

"If you get to the library later," she said, "look this up."

Momma put on her seat belt and started the car. Everyone stepped back, but Momma backed the car up and only grazed the clothesline pole. She pulled forward and started down the drive. She cried. Dad cried, and before I knew it, I was crying too.

It looked like a parade. Momma drove slowly down the driveway and the rest of us walked along beside the car, waving and wishing her good luck. She'd be home later in the afternoon, but this day had been a long time in coming. We marked it.

Possibly Momma couldn't take the sentiment any longer. She put her foot down and sped up onto the blacktop.

Dad, Kenny, Little Man, Charity, and I stood and waved until the car disappeared over the rise. We turned and started back to the house. Dad asked to see the paper Momma had given me.

It read: *bonobos*.

"What does it mean, Dad? Do you know?"

"I think you might want to look it up for yourself," he said. "But I think it means that your momma is trying to understand you better."

Each of us needed to prepare for our first day of something totally new. Momma had left for school. Thanks to Gerry, Charity had a commission painting a mural for the library until she left for art school in St. Paul the following year. Dad and Kenny started at the lumberyard. As for me, I worked with Twitch and lugged Little Man along every step of the way.

I thought about what somebody would see if they drove down the road just then. Two queer girls holding each other's hand, my free hand gripping Little Man's sticky hand, and Kenny Hollister on the other side of Little Man. Dad walked on ahead of us. I hoped anybody who saw and knew us and our story would know we were a family.

Dear Reader,

Thank you for reading Nancy J. Hedin's *Bend*!

We know your time is precious and you have many, many entertainment options, so it means a lot that you've chosen to spend your time reading. We really hope you enjoyed it.

We'd be honored if you'd consider posting a review—good or bad—on sites like **Amazon, Barnes & Noble, Kobo, Goodreads, Twitter, Facebook, Tumblr,** and your blog or website. We'd also be honored if you told your friends and family about this book. Word of mouth is a book's lifeblood!

For more information on upcoming releases, author interviews, blog tours, contests, giveaways, and more, please sign up for our weekly, spam-free newsletter and visit us around the web:

Newsletter: tinyurl.com/RiptideSignup
Twitter: twitter.com/RiptideBooks
Facebook: facebook.com/RiptidePublishing
Goodreads: tinyurl.com/RiptideOnGoodreads
Tumblr: riptidepublishing.tumblr.com

Thank you so much for Reading the Rainbow!

AnglerFishPress.com

ANGLERFISH PRESS

AN IMPRINT OF RIPTIDE PUBLISHING.

ACKNOWLEDGMENTS

I have wanted to be a writer since I was a child. My love of writing and books was fostered by my maternal grandmother, Amanda Tall. She was a teacher and she proofread articles and wrote the society column for her local newspaper. Incidentally, she also sold Avon, so when she called to get the news—who was home from college for the weekend, who had been confirmed and such, she also let her neighbors know that lipstick was on sale. She was a multitalented multitasker who instilled in me the value of reading, writing, and having a spiritual life. She had a robust spiritual life despite the fact she cheated at cards and scared the local police.

I stand on Grandma's shoulders and on the shoulders of my parents, Edwin and RoJean Hedin. They worked the hardest types of jobs to give me a bigger dream, a brighter future, and a better life than they had themselves. They both knew how to tell a story. I was lucky as the youngest of five children. There was more money, a bigger house, and a freer world as I was growing up. This circumstance of birth order meant that my siblings said I was a spoiled brat. They were right. I stand on the shoulders of Kathy, Lin, Michael, and David because they cared for me into adulthood even though as the baby of the family I had more opportunities than they did. Thank you, Mom, Dad, Kathy, Lin, Michael, and David.

The folks who make jokes about in-laws have never met mine. Jack and Mary Roeder are the real-life people about whom the Hallmark Hall of Fame stories are written. They model hospitality, generosity, Godliness, and good humor. They have raised their children to be kind, thoughtful, and hardworking citizens. I couldn't be more fortunate than to have married into the Roeder family and found another place to call home.

Thank you, Kent Haruf. I never met you, but your novels make me feel like writing stories is a sacred profession. Heartfelt gratitude to novelist Alison McGhee, who was my second reader for my thesis. It was truly an honor to have you read my work, because your work has entertained and inspired me for years. Likewise, thank you to novelist, Ellen Hart, for her encouragement to a fledgling writer and the example she set with her great writing and work ethic. Thank you to Pam Carter Joern for her novels and encouraging me to pursue an MFA at Hamline University.

The Hamline MFA program taught me to write better and faster, and gave me a community of writers and teachers who graciously spurred each other on to make our best work and live a creative life. My most intimate community of students included: Wendy, Julie, Ryan, Steve, and Gretchen. I offer special thanks to Barrie Jean Borich, who was my first instructor at Hamline. She inspired hard work, wide reading, and deeper thinking than I had ever been challenged to do previously. A good grade from her meant something. My thanks to Mary Rockcastle for seeing potential in my work and admitting me to the program even though I did not have a bachelor's degree from a qualifying university. Thanks to Deborah Keenan, who could teach anyone to love poetry and believe they might be able to change the world by writing it. Thanks to Mary Logue for showing me that an understanding and a way of organizing plot was a quick path to a first draft. Thank you to Sheila O'Connor for her work trying to get thick-headed writers like me to see the nuances of point of view. I still slip, but I am learning more with each thing I write and read.

Thanks to Patricia Weaver Francisco for guiding me through my thesis and the development of a writing process. Your creative process class should be a requirement for all creative writing students and even people who might wander in off the street. It is a valuable self-inventory and opportunity for the most conscious type of work production.

I could not have written my novels and completed the MFA program while also working full-time without the support of my colleagues at Ramsey County Mental Health Crisis Program. My team, in its many incarnations, has been the best team I could have asked for. They had my back when my head was being pulled in so many directions. Thank you Brian, Marcie, Madonna, Judy F., Sharon, Colonel Johnson, Amy, Rick, Jamie, Adrienne K., Nick, Merry, Willie, Mary Jo, Adrienne P., Maria, Karen, Barbara, Dave, Karalee, Susan, Judy L., Sally S., Sally V., Tera, Chuck, Colleen, and dearest

Mona, who hired me and mentored me although I never wore a dress to work again after that interview.

The day my agent, Ella Marie Shupe, emailed me to say she wanted to represent my work was one of the most exciting days of my life. Then, when I actually talked to her on the phone and saw that she got my work, knew my work, and wanted to champion my work, I felt sorry for any writer who didn't have her as an agent. Ella Marie and Sharon Belcastro of the Belcastro Agency have given me great guidance in my writing and have worked so very hard to find a place for my work. They both helped me keep writing—I completed two more novels while working with them—and they kept me believing that it was possible to find a publisher for my books.

Thank you to Riptide Publishing for publishing my book. I am particularly in debt to Sarah Lyons, Rachel Haimowitz, May Peterson, Alex Whitehall, and Amelia Vaughn, who shepherded my book into its final form. L.C. Chase and Natasha Snow made some sketchy ideas into a stunning cover. Riptide's gifted staff has treated me with great kindness, support, and professionalism. They have made this book better. Thank you.

Finally, the thrill of all this still takes a far off second place to the blessing of my wife and best friend, Tracy Roeder, and our daughters, Sophia and Emma. There is no greater accomplishment in my heart than the gift of being a family. It is that steadiness and continuous love that allows me to create and tell stories. Thank you, all.

ABOUT
THE AUTHOR

Nancy Hedin completed her MFA at Hamline University in St. Paul, Minnesota. Her work has been published in *Sleet Magazine, The Minnesota Women's Press, The Lake Country Journal, The Phoenix, The Midway/Como Monitor,* and *Rock, Paper, Scissors.* She has been a pastor, a bartender, and a stand-up comic, and currently works as a crisis social worker. She lives in St. Paul, with her wife and daughters.

Website: nancyhedin.com
Twitter: @njhedin1
Facebook: facebook.com/nancyhedinWRITES

Enjoy more stories like
Bend
at RiptidePublishing.com!

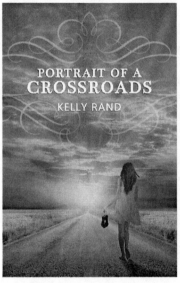

Portrait of a Crossroads
ISBN: 978-1-62649-011-6

The Beginning of Us
ISBN: 978-1-62649-105-2

Earn Bonus Bucks!

Earn 1 Bonus Buck for each dollar you spend. Find out how at
RiptidePublishing.com/news/bonus-bucks.

Win Free Ebooks for a Year!

Pre-order coming soon titles directly through our site and you'll
receive one entry into a drawing for a chance to win free books for
a year! Get the details at RiptidePublishing.com/contests.

AN IMPRINT OF RIPTIDE PUBLISHING.